The Changeling

PARANORMAL ROMANCE

THE CHANGELING

A Sweet Romance Novel

MADELINE ARCHER

Romania Books; Indie Artist Press

Paranormal Romance:
The Changeling -
A Sweet Romance Novel
Published by Romania Books
an Imprint of Indie Artist Press
Eagle Mountain, Utah
www.indieartistpress.com
First Edition
ISBN: 978-1-62522-073-8
copyright © 2015 Madeline Archer
All rights reserved.

October 2015

Only one person on earth sees my imagery exactly as I craft it and I often write details with him in mind. That was particularly true for this tale. From one dreamer to another, Ken, brother of my heart, this one's for you.

Time and telling have altered many tales shared in the British Isles. This is especially true regarding the legends of faery folk. Some wayward versions tell of winged imps who flit from flower to farmstead like butterflies. But true fae are a tall beautiful sort that, save the very tips of their ears, could walk among men unnoticed. This is also true for half-blooded changelings. They pass time as you or I, but their true nature isn't known to them.

PROLOGUE

November 1, 1867

Frances March hurried cautiously along the stable wall. So distracted by their conspiracy of mercy, she nearly jumped out of her shoes at the nicker of a horse. The sooner this deed was done, the better.

Pressing flat to the wall, she listened for the stableman, but heard only the muffled sound of stabled horses and the hoot of a distant owl. It was imperative that no one — upstairs *or* down — see her. She peered around the corner and watched as her sister disappeared through the hedge. Pulling her shawl tightly around her and the bundle she held, she scurried across the gardens to the library and slipped inside quietly. The head butler was waiting.

He stated rather than asked, "You're certain no one saw you . . ."

With a nod she went to warm herself by the fire, her bundle held close. The grandfather clock in the hall struck one.

Osgood checked his watch against it. He pressed, "Did you explain to your sister she must never speak of this again?"

"Yes, Mr. Osgood. As I said before, Agnes says no one would believe the truth of it anyway. She'd be ridiculed…her reputation *ruined*. And there's always the possibility she could be blamed for the other. It *is* unbelievable, no?"

"It is at that." Osgood nodded. "I scarcely believe it myself, Fanny. What about the poor still babe?"

Her eyes brimmed with tears. "Agnes will see him to the cradle and hopefully none will be the wiser. Mrs. Benton will think her *own* baby died and he'll get a decent burial. And that's pretty much the truth, isn't it? Her own son is as good as dead. Poor, poor laddie, wherever he is now." She crossed herself.

Osgood peered out into the night before locking the French doors and drawing the heavy curtains closed. "It's as it should be."

"Is it? Was it wise to switch them, Mr. Osgood? I mean, the baker and his wife —"

"— Had their child taken, with nothing to be done for it. They have *seven* living children to love, Fanny. Her ladyship has four in the grave. Five now."

Frances frowned. "Has her ladyship awakened?"

He shook his head. "Doctor Fischer administered a sedative. Lady Amelia was done out. She went to sleep believing her child alive and has no idea of the tragedy that occurred but half an hour later."

"*My poor lady.* To go through that long labor and, in the end, the babe too weak to survive." Emotion welling, Frances wiped her eyes. "What do you suppose *they* do with the babies they take?"

Osgood blinked his own sentiment away. "I can't say. My old Welsh grannie said the fae only took the sickly ones. But back then it was only legend."

"My Scottish gran told us the same," Frances said, shaking her head. "But Agnes says Libby Benton's baby *wasn't* sickly but strong and healthy. Nearly every child of the Benton's is as towheaded as their father, except for the two with the ginger hair like their mother. Agnes said Libby's babe was destined to be ginger."

Osgood went to the decanter and poured two small glasses of sherry. He handed one to her before downing his in one swallow. "Did your sister witness the switch?"

Frances sipped then shook her head. "When Agnes went to tidy the mother, she left the sleeping babe in the crib with no one to watch him. And, why would she think he needed to be watched? She helped bring the others into the world without fuss. It was minutes only that he was out of her sight. When she went back, another, with black hair, was in his place. That's when she told Libby the babe was asleep and she should rest a while. So distressed was Agnes that she ran up to the hill to find me."

He nodded. "It was fortunate she did. Another hour and everyone might have known."

"Oh yes, it *was* fortunate. Libby's husband was at the bakery mixing his dough, and the other children were sleeping up the stairs . . . one more child to such a large family brought little interest in him, you see. There was no one to witness the deed. Will you be telling Mrs. Smithson?"

"No, Fanny. No one in this household, save you and I, will know. Of course Mrs. Smithson would keep the secret if I asked her to, but that isn't necessary. We shan't burden anyone else with the truth."

Frances uncovered the bundle in her arms. Looking down, she smiled. "He's a handsome laddie, don't you think? I'm no expert, mind, but Agnes and I both suspect the babe is of mixed race. His little ears . . . "

Moving to her side, Osgood broke into a smile of his own. The little bundled boy was sleeping. He ran a gentle fingertip over the small, slightly pointed ear. "Yes, he very well could be. And yes, he's a handsome little man — dark like Master Evan was. May his soul in heaven forgive us."

The lady's maid put a reassuring hand on the head butler's arm. "He wouldn't want her ladyship's heart to be broken more than it already is. You know how he loved her."

"I do," he nodded. "As I see it, the baker's child is no more, taken away to some faery hill no doubt, never to be seen again, if the old stories are true. This little boy did not belong with the Benton family anyway. He's black-haired, for one. He'd grow being different, maybe disliked or mistrusted, even despised by his father as another man's bastard. Danny Benton is a highlander. You know how they are — with their superstitions — when they feel something isn't quite right. The child would suffer for a situation not of his making. It harms no one that he be raised a Pendry."

She nodded. "Yes, you're right Mr. Osgood. If nothing else, this is the better life of the two."

"It most certainly is. Master Evan is gone and Master John has been missing for a fortnight. Solicitors across London have been inquiring high and low for his whereabouts, but it isn't looking good, Fanny. Should anything have happened to Master John, there is no other heir living. This little man may very well become the 10th Earl of Pendry."

To the babe, Osgood leaned down and whispered, "And the family name will continue because of you. Shall we meet your mummy little sir?"

~*~

June, 1872

Having spent the better part of an hour searching, Eppa found the princess above ground at the edge of the oak orchard near the Aos Sidhe. While his worry melted away, sadness for her filled him. He crouched beside her and said softly, "Please Orlaith, don't hurt yourself this way."

Without turning she asked, "Why Eppa. *Why* did she do this to me?" A tear coursed down her cheek.

He wiped it away and shook his head. "I can't fathom her reason. Your stepsister's mind has a sickness that grows worse with each passing day."

"How *could* she do this? *How* could such horrible acts be justified? Our love was no threat to her. She killed poor John, killed him on this very spot before my eyes."

He watched with breaking heart as she dejectedly pressed her hands to the soil, as if willing them to feel what life might yet be here, where her lover's blood had spilled on snow five years before.

"And our babe, Eppa . . . *she took him away*! I've never given her cause to hate me. Why would she take every measure of happiness from me?"

"That you were born to your father's second wife is reason enough."

"My mother loved her as a *true* daughter. Until her foulness toward me, *I* loved her true. It makes no sense, this hatred." She stood and stared off in the distance. Turning back she told him, "I'm reminded of her deed each time my eyes set upon the boy. He is not to blame, but I cannot bear the sight of him."

"Aye, he's not to blame, yet he is a foul little lad. She raises him in her image, as her own." Eppa shook his head. "The boy believes himself a prince . . ."

"Her cruel enchantments make him believe it. They make him unpleasant so others will keep their distance."

"Aye," he said, taking in a breath and letting it out slowly.

Her voice cracking with emotion, she ground out, "And for what does she raise him? To pay her imagined tithe to hell when he's slaughtered!"

Eyes darting around the wood, Eppa cautioned her with a whisper. "Shhh, in the wood her eyes and ears might be anywhere. You wouldn't want her to find you pining here."

Orlaith turned away again and stared off in the distance. Her voice lowered. "You're right. She does delight in my pain. It is beyond reason that she'd revive those barbarous traditions. Sacrifices were set aside ages ago, long before our people came here. And to *kill* her changeling . . . such calculated cruelty."

Loving her completely, Eppa put his arms around her and rested his chin on her shoulder. He closed his eyes and wished it were possible to take her pain from her and carry it himself.

Orlaith leaned back against his chest. "I'm beyond believing there is good left in my sister." Turning, she faced him. "You are my dearest friend, Eppa. Papa trusted you. He trusted you as I trust you. It is that trust that compels me to ask you to find my son."

"Orlaith, please . . . only heartache waits for you down that path."

She smiled ruefully, "My heart can't possibly ache more. Find him, *please*. I know I'll never hold him in my arms. I know he will never call me mother. I only want to know he is safe and loved. Five years have passed. Not knowing is draining the life from me."

Resting his hands upon her shoulders, he looked into her eyes and vowed, "I will find him."

~*~

Orlaith turned to the rasping whisper that came from the ancient oak and cautiously drew closer. Spying Eppa, she was horrified to see her dear friend bruised and battered, his shirtfront red with blood. She hurried to his side. "Lord of All, Eppa, *what* has happened to you?"

"The queen sent her man to follow me. When I realized it, it was too late, there was nothing to do but for him to be silenced."

Her friend's beautiful eyes glistened with emotion. Eppa was a learned man, a student of Danu. Committing such violence would have torn his soul. His admission suddenly sinking in, her eyes widened. Dare she hope? She asked, "Silenced . . . . Are you saying you've found my son?"

He gave her a weary smile. "I have. He's a fine lad. The image of his father — dark like John, but there's a bit of your grandfather in him too. His eyes are the same shade as yours, silver like the lining of a storm cloud. I noticed that right off."

Orlaith's tears fell freely. Her voice choked when she ventured, "Then — then he's well cared for and loved?"

"He is. Knowing your sister, I can't imagine how he came to be in such a fine household. But it's obvious to me he's being raised by the humans as the prince he is, as a true son in a place called Pendry."

Pendry! Could it be her son had found his way to his father's own family? Stunned, she pressed her fingers to her lips. John's family name was an old one. His older brother Evan now headed the family. Was Evan raising his brother's son, his own nephew? Finding her voice, she explained all to her friend.

"Lord of All! Surely the queen was unaware of John's family . . . "

"A miscalculation, most likely. No matter. Oh this news brings me such joy, Eppa. Thank you my dearest, *dearest* friend. Thank you from the bottom of my heart." Orlaith hugged him close. Leaning back, she looked up and met his eyes. Silence filled the space as unsaid words hung in the air between them. The coppery tang of blood on this clothing came forward to her mind.

She said suddenly, "You must leave now. Oonagh will have your head for the death of her man."

"Aye, she will. She's wanted my death from the moment I refused her affections. But I *cannot* leave you, my dearest Orlaith."

Heart breaking and eyes brimming with tears, she hugged him tightly once more. Better he was gone from the Aos Sidhe. From her. He would remain alive then, unlike so many others she had loved and lost. She told him.

He said earnestly, "Come with me."

"I cannot leave the Aos Sidhe to this madness. What would my father say to my leaving, were he here?"

His voice thick with emotion, Eppa said, "He would send you away, to keep you safe. You know he would." He spoke true and she knew it.

"Perhaps. But knowing my son is near is reason enough to stay."

"I understand. I promise you, one day this madness will end and I will return." He laid his hands upon her shoulders and said, "Listen to me. Be watchful. Do nothing to bring your stepsister's ire."

"Will you do one last thing for me, please?"

"Anything."

Holding out her hand, she focused her thoughts and there appeared an inked quill and parchment. With these she quickly wrote a letter, folded it, and then pressed it to her heart. Closing her eyes, she made a wish and a circle of sparkling light surrounded the grove. An instant later, the shimmering ring shrank until it encased the letter she held. Handing it to Eppa, she said, "My sister may not know where he is, but she cannot be trusted not to hurt my son should she find him. Take this to his mother. The moment she reads it and places it near her heart, he will be protected by us both. Be happy, my dearest."

Eppa tucked the letter inside his tunic. He hugged her tightly one last time.

Orlaith felt his reluctant release and it magnified the ache in her heart. She watched him go. A last thought took her. "Eppa?"

He turned back, his brows raised in question.

"What is his name?"

He looked around to be sure his next words were not heard before saying, "Lenox, 10th Earl of Pendry."

ONE

Lenox
August, 1891

P leased with the results afforded by the syrup of acacia, I added a touch more to the *nicotiana rustica* and gave it a stir over the Bunsen burner. As suspected, the acacia was a proper binder for the tobacco. Fanny's voice at the door drew my attention.

"Excuse me Master Lenox, your mother asks that you join her in the solarium."

I loved my mother dearly but she had no mind for science and no understanding that experiments could not stop on a whim. "Is it essential that I join her this instant or may I finish my work first?"

She smiled. "You know her ladyship better than I, Master Lenox."

I chuckled. "I doubt that, Fanny. You've been privy to the workings of my mother's mind for thirty years at least." Frances March was more the essential right hand to my mother than simply a lady's maid. And one reason was that Fanny was the eldest of nineteen children and had an accountant's knack for keeping track of details. Even Mrs. Smithson, the housekeeper, herself an extremely competent woman, regularly conferred with Fanny. It was necessary to keep one step ahead, for my mother had more than the average share of diversions.

Always in sunny disposition and quick to humor, a smile accompanied the sparkle in her eyes. She added, "Then I'd have to say her ladyship wants you *immediately.*"

I turned back to my experiment and saw the ruin this temporary distraction had wrought on my adhering insecticide. Where syrup had been a moment before now sat a useless rubbery mass at the bottom of the beaker. "Please tell her I'll be along shortly."

~*~

I found Mother sitting amid the hydrangeas with Dudley looking on hopefully. As if the portly mastiff controlled her actions with his mind, she broke off a piece of her toast. Offering it to him, she warned, "Nicely, Dudley. You nearly took my fingers with the last."

Dudley let go a loud *woof* of assurance and sure enough, his next bite was gently done.

I chuckled at the exchange. "He'll soon roll through the garden like a barrel if you don't stop this constant feeding."

"There you are, Lenox. Look at you."

Following her gaze, I looked down to see a thick dusting of diatomaceous earth coating my trousers. Struck that morning by a possible cure for the aphids attacking the greenhouse, I launched right to the experiment without thought of my apron. "I'm working on a resolution to our imminent aphid problem."

She looked around. "Aphid . . . whatever are you talking about, dear? Our flowers are as healthy as ever."

Experience told me there wasn't a soul in the household who could understand something that I alone saw. It wasn't the first time I'd seen something clear as day and no one else had. That was the way of it for the whole of my life. I could tell at a glance if a person was healthy or ill by the light of vitality surrounding them. When I looked at the plants around me, I alone saw them with their life essence emanating bold glowing halos. The unhealthy plants scattered here and there had noticeably pale and weak auras. It didn't take long to deduce our greenhouse had become infested with parasites, no doubt from my mother's amaranthus caudatus newly arrived from Peru. "It's not important," I said, shaking my head. "Frances says you wished to see me?"

"Do sit, dear."

Within seconds Dudley came over to ply my mind with canine telekinesis. I patted the rotund fellow and told him silently to lie down, which he did, resting his heavy head and wet jowls upon my shoe.

"Dudley is always so relaxed around you. It's as though you both speak the same language." She poured a cup of tea and set it before me. I knew that mannerism as well as I knew my own name. Tea was the proverbial calm before the storm.

"Uh oh. What do you need me to *fix*, Mother?

"Can't I take tea with my baby boy?" she demurred. "You know how I like quizzing you on my blends."

I eyed her suspiciously. Those smiling hazel eyes sparkled back at me. No, there was more here than that. Lady Pendry had a penchant for dabbling. She dabbled in works of art by collecting new artists she *had a hunch on*, she dabbled in orchids and exotic plants, hence the aphids. She dabbled in the Royal Ascot, specifically in the creation of enormously flamboyant hats suitable for race day, and she dabbled in Indian tea blends. She also dabbled in the lives of everyone around her. Of the latter, she possessed a keen sense and could often tell at a glance if a match could be made between this person and that. Of the art, the old dear had not one whit of business sense. Nothing showed that so well as our gallery of dubious masterpieces. Fortunately, my father left a prosperous, orderly estate before he passed relatively young from a ruptured appendix.

I sipped her newest blend of tea and tasted jasmine, apple, oolong, and something else. I voiced my appreciation and sipped again, determined to identify the new flavor. "Very nice. I detect a different note, a sweeter apple? No . . . pear. You've added pear . . . and rosehips. A lovely blend, Mother. Your pinochle ladies will adore it."

She smiled. "Wonderful! I've promised them a new flavor this afternoon. I swear darling, you have the keenest senses of anyone I have ever known."

I chuckled. "Your pastimes have made me all that I am Mother — taste this tea, Lenox, smell that rose, Lenox. My senses sharpened out of self-defense. And I wouldn't have it any other way." At her laugh I asked, "So what did you need of me, exactly?" I lifted my cup. "I'm certain it has nothing to do with this."

Reaching into her pocket, she withdrew an envelope and tapped it against her hand unopened. "Your Great-Great-Uncle Charles from Selkirk has passed."

"I wasn't aware I had a Great-Great-Uncle Charles in Selkirk."

"No? I'm certain I've mentioned him, he's on my mother's side of the family. The Carter side? Well, it wasn't *always* Carter. They thought it prudent to change the name from MacArtair to Carter during the Clearances."

"That was wise." Though she'd said otherwise, I had no idea we'd had family in Scotland, let alone one involved in the Lowland Clearances. As anyone schooled in England's history knew, the agricultural revolution displaced both Highland and Lowland Scots. The clan system had its back broken by the crown and in seventy years it was all but gone. Anglicizing the family name may have saved them.

She explained, "As his heir, you'll need to see to his estate. I used to holiday there as a girl, I'm sure I've told you." I shook my head. She continued, "Well, it's a charming old place and I shouldn't wish to sell it. But I'll leave that to you. Perhaps we could place an estate manager there next spring."

Osgood suddenly found us. "Wicks has brought the carriage around, Master Lenox."

I looked at my mother. Her shrug suggested our coachman clairvoyantly determined I'd be leaving shortly. Tamping down my exasperation, I turned to the man, and said, "Thank you, Osgood. Please see that Wicks has a proper meal before we leave. I will need time to pack."

The butler tipped his head, and said, "I should tell you, Master Lenox, young Mr. Potts has your bags packed. Both he and your belongings are on the coach."

Mother chimed in, "I'll have your trunks sent on. I'm afraid you won't be back for a while dear. Settlings things will take some time."

My previous exasperation no longer contained, I turned back to her ladyship. "Mother, *really*."

"I knew you'd go as soon as you'd heard you were needed there. The head of an ancient estate of that size must fulfill his duties. *Noblesse oblige*, dear. The harvest is nearing. It's already the end of summer and the family sponsors an autumn festival. With Uncle Charles gone, they will need to be seen to."

I looked at the fading auras of the hollyhocks behind her. Unchecked, the solarium's aphids would have everything dead by spring. I said, "I have experiments to finish before I go."

Waving a hand, she said, "I'm sure they're nothing so large Osgood can't delegate the task to someone." She cast him an eye.

Quite used to this after so many years, Osgood asked me if I had someone from the staff in mind.

I scanned the diminishing plant auras around me and let out a breath. I didn't. Not ten minutes ago I had a resolution plotted for the impending blight. That mental formula had evaporated like frost under the sun. I shook my head. "Thank you Osgood, but don't bother. I'll finish upon my return. Please inform Potts that he'll need to make room up top for my equipment."

"Yes, Master Lenox."

I explained to Mother that if I had to be in the Scottish Lowlands for an undetermined period of time, I would, at the least, collect native plant specimens for my studies.

My mother turned her cheek for a kiss, which I gave. She said "Write of your discoveries, darling, and I shall share them with my rose club. They simply love when you share something fascinating with us."

"I certainly will."

"Now run along and gather your things."

I got the sudden impression my mother simply wanted me gone and her distant Uncle Charles made for a convenient excuse to that end. The envelope clutched tightly in her hand suggested I might be right.

~*~

Lady Amelia Pendry stood at the window. She waited for the coach to pass the gate then unfolded the ominous letter that arrived the night before. She read it again:

My Dear Lady Pendry,

I know you have been in contact with his mother. No matter. We ride on October 31st and he will ride with us.

Queen Oonagh

Her hand dipped inside her bodice and withdrew another note she'd kept close to her heart for nearly twenty years.

Dearest Lady Pendry,

Today, at long last, my search has ended. My heart could burst with joy. We both hold a dear child, our child. His father, your husband's brother John, was murdered and the babe taken from my arms the night he was born. I know not how he came to be with you, but I am grateful, truly grateful he has his true and loving family to raise him. You are able to see him safely brought to manhood and I am not. I leave him to your tender care. Never reveal he is of both worlds — human and fae — the truth might harm him. And you must keep this letter close always. The glamour I've laid upon it will keep you both safe.

Orlaith

Amelia knew this day would come. Twenty years ago she woke to discover the letter on her pillow and it confirmed what she'd always known

— her son wasn't hers. Not from her body perhaps, but certainly he was hers in her heart. Folding the edge-worn parchment, she tucked it back inside her garment.

She couldn't have loved Lenox more than when she held him to her breast that first time and felt a mother's love and devotion. It didn't matter that his ears had the slightest pointed tips that declared he was both human and fae. All that mattered was he needed her to be his mother and her arms were no longer empty. She remembered when he looked at her with those beautiful gray eyes, so much like her dear Evan's pale blue.

She read Queen Oonagh's letter again, then crumpled it in a tight fist. Lenox was *her* son and no faery queen would take him. Not even if it meant her life..

TWO

I woke to a light rap on the roof of the coach. A moment later, my manservant opened the door, and said, "Master Lenox, sir? We've arrived at the inn."

As I didn't know what to expect at the Carter manor house, I'd decided to dine at the first inn we found on the edge of Selkirk proper. I grabbed my cramping calf and massaged hard, suddenly aware of the cost of my prolonged confinement. Having met a downpour north of Harrogate, I'd had half my precious equipment loaded inside the coach rather than take a chance it be ruined up top. It made for a very cramped ride. *Damn, that smarts.* Through gritted teeth, I said, "Excellent. I don't think my legs can take much more."

Potts held the door open while I unfolded myself from the carriage.

"You look terribly uncomfortable, if I may say so, sir," he said. "Shall I put your equipment up top again so you won't have to go the rest of the distance cramped like this?"

I looked at Wicks, dressed in sodden wool with the tip of his numb nose red and dripping. The awning above had done little to keep his half of the seat dry. I shook my head. "Not half as uncomfortable as you and Wicks, I'd wager. Go dry yourselves by the fire and have a warm meal." I gestured them inside. "This can be sorted out before we travel on."

"Yes sir."

He no sooner replied when thunder rumbled overhead and the clouds opened again. The storm showed no signs of letting up. My equipment would stay where it was.

Wicks pulled us close to the shrubbery to shield the horses, and we hurried up the cobbled path to MacPhee's Peg. Above the door, the wind-blown shingle sported an old battered peg leg. I didn't wonder long about that, for inside the barman met us — MacPhee, I presumed. The man had himself a black-lacquered prosthesis for a left leg, the tip of which was carved in the shape of a stag's foot. He greeted us genially over the din. Within seconds my men were seated near the hearth and I was placed beside the iron-belly stove.

A young freckled girl of no more than twelve appeared at my elbow with a slate in her hand. After greeting me, she squinted nearsightedly at her slate, and haltingly read the first offering on the menu, "Today we ha' a de-li-ci-*ose*, de-li-ci-*us*, deli-*shus* bridie an' tattie pie w' onions." The rest was recited by rote, "We also ha' Cullen skink an' bannock. My gran says we ha' a bit o' smoked haddie left too, but if yer wantin' the haggis, we ha' no more today."

Struggling with the images her words brought to mind, I settled on the pie. Tipping my head to the hearth, I told her, "My wet fellows there, please see to them on my tab."

A short while later, well-fed and satisfied, I finished my ale and considered the sky through the diamond-paned windows. The north road had been rutted and ill-tended for the last quarter of my journey. I could only imagine what lie ahead was worsened from the heavy downpour. I contemplated taking rooms here for the night, but my thoughts were interrupted by a blood-curdling yowl rising above the tavern noise. It came from upstairs and the dining hall ceased its racket as though all sound was magically wiped from the building — not so much as a fork clanked against a plate. The abrupt silence preceded the cry of a new baby wailing with its first breath of air.

MacPhee quickly hobbled up the steps and returned several minutes later wearing a grin from ear to ear. Several patrons applauded, leading me to assume the barman had just become a father. He ducked into the kitchen. A second later an older woman followed him back out, wiped her hands on her apron, and dashed up the steps. Now behind his bar, MacPhee was laying out a row of shot glasses. He called for the freckled girl, "Penny! Yer mam's given ye a baby brother. Come pass out th' whiskey! I ha' a *new* son, good

17

people! Drinks on th' house, all 'round!"

The customers cheered.

Shortly after, an angel descended the staircase. I lost the ability to breathe as an unidentifiable tingle swept me from head to toe. It was obvious she'd been involved in the drama above for she arched her back wearily. She rolled down her sleeves and buttoned her cuffs. MacPhee slid a glass of ale her way and she broke into an extraordinarily beautiful smile. That very instant, Cupid speared my heart with an arrow.

She was quite fair with skin like fine oriental porcelain and features feminine and delicate. She was willowy and tall. Not as tall as I, but taller than most women of my acquaintance and several of the men here, and I briefly wondered if she owed her height and coloring to Viking blood from the northern conquests generations before. I couldn't determine the color of her eyes from where I sat, but her hair was so light a shade of blond my eye had to strain to be sure it wasn't white. It was braided and in that plait, fell well below her hips. Unbound it might very well come close to the floor. The curl at the end and the sweat-damp ringlets faming her face suggested a natural wave. A fanciful image took me as I imagined what it might be like to sink my hands into the moonlit silk. She laughed at something someone said, and the genuine sound made me smile. Hoping for an introduction, I went toward the bar. Unfortunately she turned and went back up the stairs with young Penny racing ahead.

A broadly smiling MacPhee said, "Wha' can I get fer ye, sir?"

It took a moment to realize he was speaking to me. Returning to a previous thought, one I'd put aside before I saw the fair maiden, I said, "I'm thinking if that rain persists, it may be in my best interest to stay the night."

The man scratched his chin. "Och. I'm sorry t' say I canna gi' ye anythin' tonight." He tipped his head toward the full common room. "Ye see, we're th' last stop 'afor Glasgow, and th' best stop before Edinburgh. This heavy storm ha' forced many t' stay o'er. I've not so much as a bench free, just th' chair ye've been sittin' in. Normally I'd send ye to Marten's stable, but I know fer a fact there's two families sleeping in th' one empty stall. Indeed,

I'm sorry sir."

"Well then, that's that. I'll square the tab." I paid the man a generous tip. "And that's for your new son."

His face lit up. "Thank ye fer that, sir. If I may ask ye, where are ye headed?"

"To settle the nearby estate of my great-uncle."

"Estate...surely yer no' auld laird Charlie's kin?"

"If you're referring to Charles Carter, yes, he was my uncle."

MacPhee looked me over, a flicker of doubt glinting in his eyes. "He was laird o' the glen. As red as a fox he was, well into his last days."

"On my mother's side."

"Ah." He nodded and said, "Well, yer not half an hour from there. Even in th' rain." He then set two glasses on the bar and poured me a jigger of whiskey in each. To my surprise he slid one to me and kept one for himself. He raised to me, and said, "To auld laird Charlie's memory, an' t' *you* sir, the new laird. It may not be easy fer an outlander to find himself at Carterhaugh, but good people they are. Ye can count upon that."

I had no time to ask what he meant, for his freckle-faced daughter came down the stairs and said, "Papa, Mam's askin' fer ye. She says gran's worrid th' faeries will take him because ye forgot to count wee Duncan's fingers an' toes. But I did t' be sure, Papa. They're all there. All o' them."

MacPhee laughed. He tossed his glass back, then wheezed, "O'course they are, my darlin' girl! Tha's just one o' yer gran's auld Highland superstitions. An' this is no' th' highlands. Come lassie. Watch th' door an' call me doon if ye need me."

A moment later, I had the opportunity to ask the girl an important question. "Penny?"

"Aye, sir?"

"The pretty lady who helped bring your brother into the world, do you know her name?"

"Aye, sir, I do. Her name is Janet Roxburgh." Penny looked around, and then to me, whispered, "My gran says Janet's a *true* witch."

~*~

Sure enough, MacPhee was right. My uncle's estate was just outside of Selkirk proper, and the ride took us no longer than twenty-five minutes and that over a sorry road. A single coach light shone at the door and no servant came forth, but then I wasn't expected. Keeping step with Potts under the umbrella, I made it to the door somewhat dry. Under my direction, he ran back to the coach and it disappeared 'round back to stable the horse and see to my luggage. The door was bolted. I rang the bell. A man in his dressing gown met me at the door, opening it only a crack and standing just behind it.

"Aye?"

Deciding we'd do our formalities out of the rain. I took a step inside.

He backed up, surprise on his face. "Here now. Who are ye t' be calling at this hour?"

"I'm Charles Carter's heir."

His mouth and eyes went as round as saucers. "Oh, *forgive* me, sir. I wasna expecting ye, ye see."

I nodded. "That makes the two of us, Mr — ?"

He straightened. "Munro, sir, Gilroy Munro."

"I am Lenox Pendry." He gave me the same flicker of doubt MacPhee had. Apparently a man's coloring gave legitimacy here in the lowlands. I added, "Great-uncle Charles was uncle to my mother, her mother's brother."

He bowed, "Yer lairdship, I'm dreadful sorry not t' have th' house turned out fer ye. Had I but known . . . . "

I waved it away. He hurried to the servant's bell and pulled the cord enthusiastically. Within moments, the foyer filled with servants from young to old, all dressed for bed. I found that odd, since it wasn't half past ten. That wasn't all I found odd. I was struck by the similarities. The servants here were as compact and sturdy as Shetland ponies, with the same facial features. Half of them were obviously related.

A slight elder woman wearing an old-fashioned night cap came forward.

She was out of breath, one hand pressed hard to her chest. Munro raised a bushy brow at her, and said, "And this is Mrs. Frew, the housekeeper, yer lairdship. She's under the weather and is *advised* to rest."

Noting the housekeeper's feeble aura, I deduced this frail old woman was sicker than anyone here knew.

She said weakly, "I wouldna' miss the new laird's coming, Mr. Munro. The sod would have to be o'er me fer that." To me she curtseyed with effort, and said, "Welcome *home*, yer lairdship. Please forgive this auld woman. I'll be back on my feet in a day or two."

Munro rushed to take her arm that she might straighten. Weak or not, the smile of welcome in her eyes was sincere.

"I'm very pleased to meet you, Mrs. Frew. Now please, take yourself back to bed. We've time enough to acquaint ourselves once you're feeling well." I gave her an encouraging smile and laid my hand on her arm. I didn't miss the flicker of surprise on her face, nor her head to toe perusal that followed.

"Thank ye, yer lairdship."

To the closest footmen, I said, "Please assist Mrs. Frew to her room."

They hurried forward and walked her down the hall. I watched them go, Mrs. Frew's aura nearly invisible between the healthy glow of the young men at her side. I felt she was never going to be back on her feet. Indeed, it struck me that she might not be with us much longer.

Munro broke me from my gloomy thoughts. "If I may I ask, did yer manservant come with ye, sir?"

"He did, and my coachman as well. I suspect they're at the service entrance."

With a nod, Munro turned to the servants and told them, "As ye see, our new master, his lairdship, the Earl of Pendry has arrived. Ye are t' see t' his coomfort. His servants are t' be found rooms for th' night, and we'll sort them out in th' morning."

"Follow me yer lairdship, I'll take ye t' yer rooms. I assume ye'll be wanting Laird Charles's auld rooms? Lord rest 'im."

I followed him up the stairs. "Any clean and comfortable room will do tonight, Munro. And please see to a hot bath."

"Aye, sir. Right away. I'll have th' water brought up from the kitchen. There's been no time t' properly heat the tanks, I'm sorry t' tell ye."

"A shallow tub will be fine for tonight. You'll find my needs simple."

"Aye, sir."

~*~

A shallow bath and a fine peaty scotch soon had me relaxed and warmed inside and out. I took myself to bed, my mind happily immersed in the vision of the ethereal beauty I'd seen at MacPhee's inn. *Witch indeed.* I chuckled. *You've certainly bewitched me, lovely lady.*

THREE

Sensing a presence in the room, I opened my eyes to discover a young chambermaid, her apron bulging with kindling. She knelt at the hearth and softly raked the coals.

"And who comes to tend my fire this morning?"

She squeaked in surprise as she jumped to her feet and whirled about, and then just as fast went back to her knees to gather up the twigs that had fallen everywhere. She quickly prattled off an apology from her place on the floor, "I'm Winnet, yer lairdship. I'm *so* sorry, sir. What a goose I am, jumpin' out o' my skin like tha. Fer an instant, I thought auld Master Charlie had come back t' haunt th' room!"

I chuckled.

In short order she had a cheery fire going. "The fire is burning hot now, th' room will be warm shortly. I'll send yer man t' ye straightaway, yer lairdship." And with that, the fast-talking girl hurried out the door.

Potts entered a moment later with my white shirt held carefully over one arm and the rest of my garments over the other. These he laid out upon the end of the bed. "Good morning, sir. I've borrowed an iron and pressed your things to remove the travel creases." He then found my shoes and taking the brush from his pocket, proceeded to buff them to a shine.

Curious, I asked, "So how did you and Wicks fair last night?"

"Oh, it's a fine place, sir. Not as grand as Pendry, but grand in its own right. You can't see a thing out the windows for all the morning fog, but I'm told the countryside is lovely. That fog is as thick as Mrs. Comstock's pea soup, it is."

Now *that* was impeccable imagery. Our cook made a pea soup that could stand a spoon. "And the staff? Many differences?"

"Not to me, sir, but then my granddad on my mam's side was himself a Scotsman. And a superstitious man he was too. They seem to be fine people here, sir. Odd with their quirks, as all Scotsmen are, but friendly and efficient, as far as I can tell. I think you'll find the accent takes some work, the speak too, if you get my meaning, sir. I was told they planned to serve you woodcock for your breakfast. And so you know, sir, they mean toast with shirred eggs and smoked fish on top."

I laughed over the rumbling sensation that caused in my belly. "Let's hope I learn quickly, Potts. I'll be here a while." The night before, I'd asked him to inquire about the blond witch, though not using those words. "Did you learn anything about the MacPhee's pretty midwife?"

He helped me into my jacket and smoothed the fit across my shoulders. "That was the odd thing, sir. I mentioned we'd stopped and took our supper at MacPhee's Peg. I mentioned the innkeeper had a new baby boy and I learned the new mother has ties here; she's the groundskeeper's younger sister. Then I asked in a roundabout way about the young blond midwife attending her."

"And?"

"Not a word, sir. Where they were upfront and sociable just a minute before, the lot of them shut their gobs tighter than clams. There's one maid I might do better with. She's a friendly, chatty sort."

"And that would be Winnet."

I saw his surprise in the mirror. I also saw his attraction. "Yes sir, it is. MacPhee is her uncle by marriage, as a matter of fact. All smiles and sunshine, that Winnet." His smile went from ear to ear.

And the thought of finally having my answers made *me* smile.

~*~

Munro met me in the dining hall with a footman in tow. The latter set a tray before me and removed the silver dome. He tipped his head, took one step back, turned on his heel, and left.

Munro said, "Good morning, yer lairdship. I hope ye'll enjoy yer breakfast, simple as it is. We've not much here at th' moment, sir, just what is in th' larder. If there's anything ye're wanting, our cook Mrs. Nevin can have it ordered straightaway. The poor embarrassed woman is worrit ye might find her incapable o' presenting a decent meal, after such a simple breakfast. I assure ye, yer lairdship, Mrs. Nevin is an *accomplished* cook. The auld laird always went on with praise fer his suppers."

I looked at my plate of Scotch woodcock. It was a simple meal but presented like an artist's still life. I nodded. "I'm certain Mrs. Nevin will do a splendid job seeing to our meals as well as ordering whatever is necessary. Please give her my leave to do so and have the bills brought to me." Tasting the dish, I added, "And do tell her I've never tasted better Scotch woodcock."

He smiled. "Aye sir, I shall. Would ye like me to schedule a meeting with Hamish Ennis, sir? He's th' grounds keeper here."

"I would. Actually Munro, I'd like to meet the entire staff one at a time. Let's begin with the least position and go from there."

A brief glint of surprise lit the man's eyes, yet was absent from his voice when he asked, "Ye wish t' meet the scullery maid and the stable boys, yer lairdship?

I nodded.

Apparent surprise widened his smile. He bowed his head. "Aye sir, as ye wish."

~*~

I'd met a full third of the staff before Winnet came into the study midday. We talked for a time wherein I learned the life histories of several people on the staff, including hers. Indeed my impression of the night before bore out. No fewer than nine siblings saw to the household, from scullery maid to first footman, and every one of them a grown child of Mrs. Nevin. Winnet herself was Mr. Ennis's daughter and her brother Samuel had been my uncle's coach and stableman. In many ways Winnet reminded me of a young Francis March — every bit as pleasant and personable, her finger on the pulse of the household.

I asked, "Has Mrs. Frew been seen by a physician lately?" The cessation of Winnet's extroverted accounting was so immediate I wasn't sure she'd heard my question. I repeated, adding, "I'm concerned. The housekeeper does not look at all well."

"No, she's not, sir. But she's auld and auld ones are set in their ways." She drew a breath and I saw her mind working.

Before she "shut her gob tighter than a clam" I prodded, "How is Mrs. Frew set in her ways? Are you saying she's never seen a doctor for her condition?"

Winnet shook her head.

Tight as a clam, indeed. I ventured a guess as to the reason for it. "I'll not see an old woman's health fail for want of coin. Please tell Mr. Munro to send for the doctor."

Her eyes grew wide. "Oh no sir, I didna mean t' imply she's no been *treated*. It's o nly that th' person was called away to assist a difficult birth an' Mrs. Frew has run out of her medicines."

I felt an answer coming to the question I hadn't yet asked. "Who's treating her?"

"I hesitate t' say, yer lairdship. Like I've said, th' auld ones are —"

"— set in their ways. Yes, they often are, Winnet. Now, who exactly is treating Mrs. Frew?"

"Janet Roxburgh, sir."

Hiding my excitement, I simply nodded. "And this woman is a physician?"

No sooner did I ask when I could see worry in her eyes. MacPhee said an outlander would not have an easy time here. Insight came to me. This chatty maid was worried I'd sack old Mrs. Frew for believing in old wives tales and choosing a country midwife over a doctor. My insight was born out when Winnet assured me. "Uh, no sir, Janet is skilled in th' *auld* healing ways."

Another way of saying witch? I gave Winnet a reassuring smile. "I take no issue with old ways Winnet. I only want Mrs. Frew to get good care."

Her relief was instantaneous. "Yes, sir."

We talked of other things a bit longer then I asked calculatingly, "How often does Mrs. Frew get her treatments from Mrs. Roxburgh?"

"Oh Janet's no' marrit, sir. Before she was called away t' tend my Auntie Rose — she's marrit to Ross MacPhee, who owns th' tavern on th' edge of town where ye stopped — anyway, my auntie was havin' a hard time, ye see." Winnet spilled forth a lengthy account harvested from family gossip, then finally gave me what I wanted to hear when she said, "Janet comes t' see Mrs. Frew at least every other day."

This was turning into a splendid day after all. I nodded. "Thank you for the explanation, Winnet. Please send Mr. Munro in. I'll have him send a note to Miss Roxburgh to let her know I'll pay whatever she requires to continue treating Mrs. Frew."

Winnet shot to her feet. "Yes, sir. Uh . . . yer lairdship?"

"Yes?"

"Janet willna take yer money. That's no' her way, ye see."

I smiled. "Alright, then I'll simply ask her to come as soon as she's able."

"Yes, yer lairdship."

I stopped Winnet as she opened the door. "So who do I meet with next?"

She poked her head around the corner. "Burley Nevin, sir. He's th' second footman."

"Please send him in."

She smiled with her curtsey and left the room.

FOUR

As it was with Pendry, the relationship between land holder and tenant here at Carterhaugh was one of long-standing symbiosis. Both estates existed on rents, those portions gleaned from production of wool and grain from tenant farmers as well as the profits of two small textile mills on the river Tweed in Galashiels.

My first week in the Scottish Lowlands was spent becoming acquainted with the workings of the Carter holdings. Uncle Charles was loved by his people and was considered a fair and just laird who, more times than not, moved among them as a benefactor. I listened to posthumous praise of the man at every door — and how he regularly bestowed generous wedding and baptismal gifts and so on.

My uncle oversaw the enormous harvest's end celebration and the smaller Mummers' Fair. The latter saw him personally run the first head of cattle through the Beltane fires. Fancy that. In short order I gained deeper insight and appreciation for my mother's family out of ordinary pastimes. Apart from inherent generosity, the Carters were known for their eccentricity. Apparently Uncle Charles's father, Dunnley, had this unconventionality in spades. The elders here fondly remembered him for the pocket of sweets he regularly doled out to them as children, but it was Dunnley's pet raven, Rob Roy, that brought him renown. They told me the bird spent the day perched atop the old man's flat-crowned hat, shatting down the back.

From the extensive library I discovered the family was older than Selkirk itself. Their ancient Selgovae tribal roots were planted prior to the coming of the Romans and dug deep into Lowland turf thereafter. It didn't take long to discover the Carter lands and the people on them had lives as intricately woven as Scottish plaid.

Twenty-seven ledgers into my inquiry, I read how rogue clans fought one another and be damned to those between them, the tenants of Carterhaugh included. And how, during the worst of the reivings, laird Alpin MacArtair kept all safe through payment of substantial bribes and large tracts of relinquished land. Later, during the first King James's Pacification of the Borders, these same sacrifices allowed Alpin to look after his people while smaller estates around them were broken, and tenant and aristocrat alike were deported to Ireland, Australia, and the Americas. That he used his own wealth to safeguard security during these dark times was quite admirable, really. It did much to explain the fealty I encountered here.

Another ledger clearly explained how the estate had an upturn in prosperity with the coming of the tweed mills some sixty years prior. Dunnley Carter, despite being daft enough to cover himself in bird droppings, speculated well when he bought into a one-hundred-to-one scheme.

Because Munro's father had been head butler during this time, I asked him what he knew about this speculative business.

He explained, "Oh, my father often talked about that brilliant scheme, sir. Ye see, auld laird Dunnley took advice from th' acting sheriff. That was Sir Walter Scott at the time. Auld Scott had connections t' the mill barons of th' west an' they felt th' idea sound."

Sure enough, Munro's tale matched the ledger. The one-hundred-to-one scheme played out and lands once sold in desperate times were returned to the holdings.

From Barnabas Simms, the acting estate manager, I learned that Uncle Charles handled his own management for no other reason than how personable he was. According to Simms, Uncle Charlie was "a noble soul wi' a common touch."

Seven years earlier, holdings in Roxburghshire had been absorbed when the many enclaves comprising the whole of Selkirkshire were consolidated. The Carter holdings increased through this reordering. Proud people I knew the Scots to be, I doubted this change sat well with Randal Roxburgh who had gone from laird to squire in one stroke of a pen. Thoughts of Roxburghshire brought to mind the fair witch. Was Janet related to those Roxburghs somehow?

Running with the daydream, my mind's eye fixed upon the image of her fairly skipping down the tavern stairs. The detail was so clear I could almost see the dancing curl at the end of her moonlight braid. I was hungry to know more about her, but after a full week Janet Roxburgh remained a mystery. Inquiring among the servants gave me little to work with. Winsome Winnet revealed my elusive beauty had managed to treat Mrs. Frew four times in the past seven days without my once seeing her on the premises. Thus I decided to pay Mrs. Frew a visit.

~*~

I followed Winnet down the hall to the service quarters. Unlike Pendry and other manor houses of my acquaintance, Carterhaugh had no downstairs, where the inner workings of hearth and home took place; rather it operated with precision from the far left wing. This equally spotless portion of the manse housed the kitchen, laundry, and assorted servants' rooms. That this wing was several hundred years older than the rest led me to deduce I was seeing the original manor. An odd section it was, too. Stone arched doorways and rich dark paneling smelling heavily of lemon oil were topped with trim that sported here and there an incongruent array of carvings. Mostly these were stags and grouse of the sort seen on Swabian cuckoo clocks, but the occasional grinning gargoyle and scowling griffin perched here and there.

Winnet knocked lightly upon the housekeeper's door as she opened it a crack, and said, "Mrs. Frew, are ye awake? Mrs. Frew? His lairdship has come t' see ye."

A voice came from within, "Och, come in, *come in* girl. Dinna leave his lairdship out in th' *hall*."

The maid smiled up at me sheepishly.

I entered the cheery housekeeper's sitting room and found Mrs. Frew before the hearth with her feet on a cushion and a book in her hand. She made to rise and I bid she stay seated.

"Good day, yer lairdship." To Winnet she said, "Be a good lass and bring us some tea."

Winnet curtseyed and left us.

She smiled and asked, "How may I help ye, sir?"

Though not at optimal health, she still looked surprisingly hale. Her aura had visually improved in strength tenfold. I said anyway, "I've come to inquire on your health, Mrs. Frew. I see Miss Roxburgh's treatments are serving you well." Taking a seat directly across from her, I lightly patted her hand.

Surprise briefly lit her wise old eyes — the same reaction I witnessed my first night here. She said, "Aye, yer lairdship, Janet knows what she's about. I hear ye've offered t' pay on my behalf. I thank ye for that, sir, but Janet's no' the sort to take coin fer her healing."

Winnet returned with a small tea service. After seeing to our cups, she left us alone. Hoping to return to the topic of the elusive witch, I commented, "Janet must be a remarkably talented healer. You appear *much* improved in a short span of days. I encountered Miss Roxburgh at MacPhee's Peg, where she stood as midwife to the innkeeper's wife."

The housekeeper smiled. "Aye, Rosie MacPhee lost four bairns between her Penny and wee Duncan. Janet saw this laddie well into the world. Had her mother-in-law not long objected t' a healer rather than a doctor, she might ha' born those other bairns as well."

"Oh?"

"Ye see, it wasn't all that long ago, no more 'n one-hundred-sixty years, since a healer was tried as a witch and burned at the stake in the highlands. Grannie MacPhee, she comes from there, aye?" She took a sip of her tea. "Och, never mind me, yer lairdship. I'm only verra fond of Rosie. She's aunty to our Winnet and a younger sister to yer grounds keeper, Mr. Hamish Ennis. Hamish was Highland born, but after his parents came here, this is where Rosie was born and raised, ye see."

I nodded and listened. We chatted amiably for a time, discussing the finer details of running the household. Her age and experience filled gaps left by the younger and less-worldly Winnet. I learned Mrs. Frew occasionally accompanied my uncle on his rounds through the parsonage. She mentioned the headmaster of the town school as an extremely educated man, once my uncle's dear friend, and "worth my trouble to meet." Then she told me about her heart. Apparently scarlet fever had as a child had done permanent damage. Occasionally this would lay her low.

I learned that four years prior, one Dr. Geevers from Edinburgh had told her to put her affairs in order, her heart was so weak he didn't expect her to live out the month. I also learned that Janet had offered to help and concocted several tinctures. Mrs. Frew's health improved within days. To this day, provided she took her prescribed daily doses, she led a strong and healthy life. Indeed, the woman's improved aura indicated the moonlit witch possessed extraordinary skill. I also learned Janet concocted these potions fresh each week. Hearing that, I couldn't help but wonder how she managed it in the dead of winter, so I asked Mrs. Frew.

"Oh, she no doubt has her ways," was the humorous reply.

I set my cup and saucer aside. "Mrs. Frew, it occurs to me that you have no issue in discussing Miss Roxburgh and her professional treatment. May I ask why the rest of the staff shies away when I've asked the same?"

Silent for a moment, she tapped her chin as if forming a response understandable to me. She said, "What makes folks tight-lipped is thinking their new English laird would ill take th' news his people still believe in th' auld ways."

I nodded and assured her. "I promise you I take no such issue, Mrs. Frew. Through my studies I have discovered the old ways often hold truths worth holding onto. This is especially true in regard to plant medicines."

"I'm thinking th' auld ways wouldn't bother a man such as yerself, sir. I could tell right off yer th' sort to understand."

I had no idea what she meant. My understanding was thin at best. Those wise blue eyes bore into me for a moment in obvious appraisal and then crinkled at the corners. Her tone was oddly light when she added, "D' ye believe in faery stories, yer lairdship?"

The only faery stories I knew came from Osgood's unusual collection of folk tales. Seeing the humor in her eyes, I played along. "Mrs. Frew, are you telling me Miss Roxburgh has wings?"

She laughed merrily. "Och *no*. She's no' a *storybook* fairy, yer lairdship. Though some say Janet *is* a true *witch*."

I was about to ask her to elaborate when Potts knocked upon the opened door. "Excuse me, Master Lenox, sir. I've readied your vasculum and duffle. Mrs. Nevin will have me tell you she has packed a bottle of ale and a lunch basket for your outing. I would add, sir, that the clouds are darker in the western sky."

I thanked him. Though I was enjoying my discussion with Mrs. Frew, it was best to end it now. I didn't want to tire her. I said, "I must be off before the Lowland weather changes on me. Again, I am pleased to see your health restored, and I'd like to continue our discussion another time."

"Of course, yer lairdship. And Janet tells me I'll be back t' my work by week's end."

I rose. Taking her hand, I said, "Take all the time you need, Mrs. Frew. It's far more important to me that your health improves. You have my permission to direct the others from your chair, if need be."

She gave me that surprised look again before breaking into a smile. "Thank ye, yer lairdship. May I say, yer verra much like auld Laird Charles. I think ye both would ha' got on."

I smiled and left her to her tea.

~*~

Glynnis Frew watched the door close after the young laird. Alone now, she called to mind events of twenty years before. A weary and worn traveler had come knocking, looking for work in exchange for a place to sleep. He appeared to be not more than forty years old and was a tall and fine-looking man with a scholarly bearing for all his tattered clothes. Kindly, Laird Charles took him in and the pair became fast friends. He soon saw the man situated in the village as the school headmaster. A handsome man, then as now, ladies from far and wide hoped to catch the headmaster's eye, but only one did just that.

Young and willful Annabel Roxburgh, only sister to the earl on the neighboring estate, met the headmaster and fell in love and soon after found herself with child. She'd hid her pregnancy from everyone. The night she went into labor, her drunken brother became outraged. In his shame, he heartlessly cast her out into the snow. She'd walked miles to get this far. It was a miracle she survived the trek to Carterhaugh at all. Her babe was born here, and Annabel named her daughter Janet Eppa Roxburgh, with both the father's name and hers, though the poor mother perished shortly after. Laird Charlie sent for the man, and how grief-stricken the headmaster had been as he keened over Annabel. Even the blind could see the love he felt for both mother and child. Earl Roxburgh refused the babe as his kin, despite all those who'd stood witness to his sister birthing the child. Soon, after the consolidations absorbed all of Selkirkshire, the earl burned the manse and killed himself. Janet was not legal heir to what was left — all she had was her mother's name to say otherwise.

Sipping her tea, Glynnis recalled the day of the funeral, when Headmaster Eppa held his hands to her in thanks. That's when she felt the rushing tingle run up her arm. She hadn't felt such since she was a girl in the highlands, but she knew it for what it was. His white-blond hair was growing silver, true, but his face held not one wrinkle more than it did the night he came knocking those many years ago. Only then did she take note of the pointed ears he obviously tried to hide. The ears on wee Janet had slightly pointed tips as well. That, and the fact he hadn't aged a day in twenty years, confirmed it to her mind. Headmaster Eppa was not of this world.

As a girl, she remembered her auntie bore a son much too soon and far too sickly to survive. She'd gone with her uncle when he placed the wee laddie upon a faery hill in the hopes the fae would take him away and make him well with their magic. He'd explained how the babe would never return, and said leaving him was the only hope for the child. Sure enough, come morning the sickly babe was gone and a hale and hearty changeling was in his place — a mixed-raced boy with slightly pointed ears. Auntie happily raised him as her own, for it meant the fae had her son and were doing the same. Owen she'd named them both.

Glynnis smiled. Many was the time she'd held wee Owen and each time he set her tingling from head to toe. It was a sensation one never forgot. The very tingle came from the headmaster's touch the day of Annabel's funeral, and the same came from Janet. Surprise of surprises, the tingling sensation also came from the hand of the new Laird of Carterhaugh. Glynnis had seen the young man's ears today and they held the slightest point at the tips, just like Owen's, just like Janet's. Perhaps Laird Lenox was a changeling, a mixed race man of fae and human blood. She wondered if he knew what he was. Her guess was no. So many of their kind never knew, and those who did never talked.

Glynnis went to her desk and taking paper and pen from the drawer, wrote:

My Dear Master Eppa,

The new laird has come at last to Carterhaugh. As you are a man of letters, I believe he would be delighted to meet you. You will find him much like Laird Charles in temperament. You might also find him more than a match for your Janet.

My Fond Wishes,
Glynnis Frew

She sealed the envelope and rang for a footman. The new laird was a fine man — neither superstitious nor close-minded. At last, a man worthy of Janet Roxburgh, and one able to restore her birthright.

FIVE

Osgood was sitting at the table in the butlery, decanting the Oloroso sherry, when voices down the hall caught his attention. Not expecting a delivery at this hour of the day, he poked his head through the doorway to find Mrs. Comstock, paring knife in hand, addressing an apple peddler who had come to the service entrance to sell her wares. Seeing it didn't immediately concern him, Osgood went back to his work. A peddler selling wares at the service entrance was a common enough occurrence, but for some reason he was compelled to listen to the exchange.

~*~

Mrs. Comstock gestured with her paring knife, and said, "I'll have you know, I'll not be spending her ladyship's good coin on apples picked too soon."

Rheumy eyes apprehensively lingering on the small steel blade, the old woman took a step backward. She rummaged in her burlap sack, withdrew a perfect apple, and handed it over. Displaying several long teeth in her smile, her words happily tumbled in a Welsh accent, "Oh ye won't *ever* foind better. Here, taste fer yerself. Take a bite o' the most delicious apple this side o' the Garden o' Eden. From what I hear, th' young master is verra fond o' apples, aye? He's sure t' love these!"

Mrs. Comstock waved dismissively, "The master is in Scotland now, and will be for some time. But even if he were standing right beside me, your apples would have to please *me* first." She sliced the fruit in two and took a loud bite. Juicy words followed, "Ooh, this is good, not too sweet. Yes. I'll take the lot. Her ladyship might enjoy a nice apple tart and custard for tea."

~*~

What is it about that peddler's voice? Listening to the exchange, a niggling recollection stayed just out of Osgood's reach. Awash with a sense of familiar and feeling unaccountably unsettled, he recorked the wine and left the butlery to join the women in their transaction. As he advanced down the hall, he got a good look at the peddler. She was old and crabbed and looked to be in advanced age. *That old peddler has been here before.* His brows drew downward as the elusive memory popped into his mind. *Twenty years ago!* Nearly twenty years had passed but she'd hadn't aged a day, in fact, she looked exactly the same. As the woman turned to leave, he hurried down the corridor, shouting, "*Stop madam*! Stop *right* there!"

Too late, the cook turned in surprise. The head butler bumped into her in his haste, sending her full apron of fruit rolling across the floor. Osgood called over his shoulder, "So sorry, Joanie!"

Mrs. Comstock's called after him. "Mr. Osgood! What in heavens are — "

He threw open the door and dashed outside. There was no one in the service yard. He ran around to the front of the building. No one. Coming back inside, he quickly apologized again to the cook, then went to find Fanny.

The lady's maid was in the laundry where he found her sewing a button on a riding glove. Checking down the hall in both directions to see if they were alone, he closed the door as a precaution. Winded, he leaned against the sink and asked breathlessly, "Fanny, do you remember the old apple woman?"

She shook her head, confused. "I'm sorry, Mr. Osgood, do I remember whom?"

"The old apple woman!" He snapped before he checked himself. "Forgive me, Fanny. The old apple woman, twenty years ago in the hedge . . . ."

Recollection coming, Fanny gasped. "The old peddler who tried to *kidnap* Master Lenox?"

Taking out his handkerchief, he blotted his brow. "The same."

"Oh, I remember." Her hands went to her cheeks. "If Arthur Brookes hadn't been trimming the verge that day, she might have *taken* the lad."

He nodded. The gardener had charged after the old woman as she pulled the struggling five-year-old behind her. Brookes had the iron hedge sheers in his hand and explained how when the old woman saw them, her eyes went round as saucers with fear. She released the boy and ran around the hedge. Brookes had been right on her heels, yet the moment he rounded the corner, she was nowhere to be seen, nor was there cover in the oat field.

Since the babe came to the household, Osgood had read everything he could lay hands on regarding the fae and their ways. He found folklore mostly, but he was of opinion that the old legends held truths, especially that the fae would try to take any child that had any of their blood. And another thing came to light again and again, that the fae did not like iron whether in the form of horseshoe nails, hedge clippers, or a steel paring knife. As far as he knew, Master Lenox with his mixed blood held no such aversion to touching iron, and often used steel tools in his studies. Lacking understanding of the complexities of it all, he frowned.

He'd been in service to this family since he came begging a meal at the kitchen door as an orphaned boy of nine. Kindhearted Lady Marjorie took him in and put him to work beating rugs and sweeping the kitchen floors. He wasn't much older than Masters Evan and John when he rose in rank to become Master Rupert's man. Having recognized a keen head for numbers and an ordered mind, Master Rupert made him head of the household staff at age thirty-two.

His eyes fixed to Lady Amelia's mended glove on the table, his thoughts straying to the men no longer here, the three he missed. They were cut from the finest cloth, and young Master Lenox, with his astounding physical similarity to Master John, and to Master Rupert himself, was as good and noble as the rest, a true Pendry if ever there was. He nodded to himself. Master Rupert entrusted him to watch over this family and that was exactly what he would do.

Fretting, Fanny said, "Our Master Lenox is a man full grown. Why ever would they come for him now?"

Osgood turned to Francis March, his accomplice in bringing a changeling here to be raised an earl. They would need to be vigilant, for apparently this drama had not come to a close twenty-four years ago. "I don't know why," he said, "but it's obvious, Fanny. They want him back."

~*~

The old woman hurried toward the open barley field and jumped the pasture gate as spryly as a girl. On the other side, away from human eyes, she drew a deep breath. A sparkling wash of glamour dissolved the visage of the old apple seller, and what remained was a shorter, non-human hob. Pleased with his mission, Billy Blin smiled. Despite the fact the young prince was a grown man now, John Pendry's people were still watching over the lad. This was good. Yes yes yes, it was, for these were dangerous times.

The young prince Lenox was naught but five years old when the queen discovered the truth — that the boy was being raised in a manner befitting the prince he was. Billy had volunteered to bring the lad to her, knowing the queen would send another if not him. He deliberately bungled the plot by attempting to take the prince in plain sight of the humans. As he'd predicted, he did not get away unmolested, as a man with hedge sheers ran to rescue the prince. Iron was deadly to magic folk and he had never been so afraid for his life as he had then. For if he died, who would stand between Queen Oonagh and dear Orlaith? Who would keep the mad queen from Orlaith's son? Eppa would have for sure, but he was gone to the north without a word or a bird for more than twenty years.

Thinking on the queen's madness, Billy's mind returned to that sad, sad night long ago. Seeing John murdered in the snow had caused Orlaith to give birth to their son. Queen Oonagh heartlessly commanded the newborn prince be taken away and a human babe brought in his stead. Billy had offered to do it for he knew she would put the newborn prince to death then and there. It broke his heart to do it, but at least he could assure Orlaith's son would be raised in safety.

With the babe in his arms, he'd called the birds of the forest and asked them to discover where he might find a human child born to a large family, hoping many children might ease the pain of losing one. As he'd hoped, a raven heard such news from a cat, who'd had it from a ewe, who'd heard it whispered from a wren, who'd seen it for herself from her perch outside a window. A hearty boy had been born nearby to a baker's wife who already had herself a very large brood. Then an owl brought news of a sickly newborn who had passed away at the home of Orlaith's lover, John Pendry. It only took minutes before Billy knew that sisters had tied the households together — midwife and maid. This small string of facts was enough to go on, and all went well because the mother at the home of John Pendry was held in high regard by her household. Aided by that affection, it didn't take much magic to tie the two events together. Magic worked its best when love and affection were involved.

Cutting through a scraggly orchard, Billy plucked a small green apple from a tree and popped it into his mouth, stem and all. His hard munching matched his troubled thoughts.

What would King Ruaraidh have said about his own daughter reviving the sacrifices, and with them all the black evil of the time before time? What would he say . . . his own grandson first banished and now intended for worse? And Maeve . . . dearest Maeve. It all would have broken her heart.

He missed her so. He'd loved that family of women. Lady Riona herself had placed the infant Maeve in his arms and asked that he watch over her daughter always. Maeve had asked the same of him when she laid the infant Orlaith in his arms. But Orlaith had never asked the same for her son. She'd never had the opportunity. Remembering, his eyes brimmed.

It didn't matter whether Orlaith had asked or not. The night he took the babe from the grove, he promised the prince he would watch over him too. And he did, surreptitiously, through the observations of the creatures that lived on Pendry lands. For several years, a peacock had watched over the boy and regularly relayed his health and happiness. As the boy grew to manhood and ventured off on his own, Billy spoke often with the young prince's horse, for no one knew the lad better.

It was the best he could do. He'd tried to watch over them all. He'd tried. His heaviest regret was not discovering Oonagh's deed in time. The helplessness surrounding Maeve's loss stuck in his heart and emotion soon brought on a runny nose that he absently wiped on his cuff. Coming too late on the scene that day, he'd not been able to save his sweet Maeve nor her good husband the king who had died just days later. Orlaith too had been given a poisonous charm, but he saved her the same fate with an enchantment of his own. His kind rarely worked magic because it was formed from their own life essence. That day he did so, and the magic was such that Oonagh could never physically harm her sister again. His tears fell freely now. Harm came in many forms. He'd saved Orlaith's life, true, but he hadn't been able to save her from the rest.

Oonagh's cruelty frightened him. He felt sorry for her, for he knew the moody child she once was. Oonagh's true mother was the result of a fae prince's dalliance with a Ban Sidhe, or as some called them, banshee — those people of unstable minds who lived and wailed upon the moors. Yes, there was something dark and unstable about Queen Oonagh, and it was growing. After she became queen, she delved deeper into the book her father had once kept under lock and key. Her continued contact with *The Black Opus* added to the poison already rooted in her mind.

Her unstable mind. His spindly fingertips absently traced the thick-healed circular scar where his ear had been. With a shudder he remembered the sound and searing pain of enchanted silver scissors snipping through his flesh. The queen's magic was terribly enhanced by dark charms. Deep in thought, Billy mumbled to himself as he walked among a flock of mossy sheep grazing in the glen.

Aside from momentarily raising their heads to see who walked among them, the ewes paid him little attention. Hobs frequented barns and stable, sharing gossip, grain, and milk, and chasing rats and weasels away in return. If Queen Oonagh ever discovered it was him who meddled in her plots, the pieces of him would be too small to bait fishhooks for sticklebacks. He must have voiced his last thought aloud, for the lone ram bleated in reply. He told it, "You're right, Master Ram. She'd *not* be happy with me. Yes, yes, yes, that is most certain."

The ram bleated a question.

Billy explained, "She plans to sacrifice the young prince."

Bleating wildly, the ram trotted after him.

"Yes it *is* terrible, *terrible*. And there are less than three months until Oonagh's Tithe." He frowned. "Foolish old barbaric ways, and all untrue, you know. She sent me to that house to be sure he was still there and he's not. I must think of something to tell her, Master Ram." Billy stopped in his tracks and glanced fearfully around the pasture to be sure no one heard. Recklessly uttered without thought, those words were dangerous. Her spies were everywhere. One never disagreed with Queen Oonagh without paying a price for perceived insolence. He cautioned the ram, "Best you keep this discussion to yourself." With that, Billy leapt cleanly over the stone wall and left pasture and flock behind.

In her madness the queen had just up and decided she wanted her own nephew to die along with the human she'd raised. Billy set his jaw. *No, no, no, never would I allow either boy that fate.* His thoughts went to Rowan, the changeling. Her charm upon him would last only until the day he turned twenty-five. If a seed of doubt was planted in the young man's mind, her enchantment upon him would weaken. *Yes yes yes.* He would wait for the opportunity to free the lad.

Taking his pointed cap from his pocket, he pulled it down past his remaining earlobe. Perhaps if the queen didn't see his intact ear, she wouldn't think to lop it off. All in all, as much as it hurt, the loss of both ears was a small price to pay to keep Orlaith and her son safe. If only he could take

Orlaith away from this sadness, but he doubted she would ever leave the Aos Sidhe.

His friend Eppa came to mind. Eppa loved Orlaith. Was it possible love could convince her to leave this place? He wondered where the gentle scholar was. If only he could sneak away to go find him, but he couldn't chance being gone. As long as madness ruled the Aos Sidhe, he could never leave Orlaith here alone. Who knew what torment Oonagh might dream up? He searched the treetops. Spying a flock of roosting starlings, he caught one's attention. The bird flew to the lowest branch over Billy's head and from there hopped to a waiting finger.

Billy told him, "I need your help, dearest. I seek my friend Eppa who may be to the north where the auld ones once lived. Please ask your fellows to search far and wide. You will know him by the glow of his essence. Go now."

The starling joined his flock in the treetop and the chittering of one-hundred-three birds came in reply. In a whoosh of wings, a great murmuration of starlings hit the sky and flew northward.

Billy came to the enchanted copse. To those unable to see the truth before their eyes, the faery hill was veiled in illusion, appearing as a grassy knoll surrounded by ancient oaks and yew trees. To magical beings, an enormous crystal dome allowed sunlight to shine on the city below. A doorway appeared with a wave of his hand. Walking through, Billy disappeared in a swirl of glitter.

~*~

Oonagh regarded each fully-opened flower carefully as she walked among the roses, silver clippers in hand. Diminished aura signaled the life of the rose had come full circle. She couldn't abide fading blooms and once had an entire plum thicket destroyed after a late-season frost caused the trees to drop their blossoms too soon. She couldn't abide fading of any sort. In fact, more than one aging woman had been banished from the Aos Sidhe court.

Thinking about them brought a frown. The faces of those courtiers — their aged and desiccated faces — hung around her court like so many withered winter apples refusing to drop from the tree. They reminded her of her own rapidly fading beauty.

A wrinkled rose brought to mind her mother Ensala, the source of this unwanted legacy. Frown deepening, Oonagh snipped the bloom from the stem and kicked it under the foliage, out of sight. When she was but four years old, her mother left for the moorlands and never returned. Her father explained that Ensala was simply too sad to stay in the Aos Sidhe, that her kind preferred the fog and lonely moors. Oonagh shrugged the memory away. She was glad for it. Ban Sidhe made unaffectionate mothers who did nothing but lament their lives. Worse, they looked old when they were young. Ensala's mixed blood had aged her quickly and she had passed this terrible trait to her daughter.

Oonagh was determined this unfortunate reality wouldn't progress. Only a few months more and she would be assured of it. Tithes could be made to hell and wishes granted for them. *The Black Opus* described how such magic was once done long ago. Ageless beauty was a wish worth a blood sacrifice.

She recalled the day she discovered the book locked behind glass doors in her father's library. When she asked him about it, he explained *The Black Opus* was written in the time before time when magical beings were as violent as the humans above ground. The book was charmed and therefore could never be destroyed. It had been burned so many times by those trying, the cover was charred black.

Intrigued by ancient magic, she'd stolen it away one night to read from cover to cover. She had every intention of returning the book to her father's cabinet but she found it all so fascinating; especially the chapter that described wishes exchanged for blood sacrifices. She had several unfulfilled wishes to rectify.

Holding power and inciting fear and awe appealed to her. *The Black Opus* was filled with powerful yet frightening things, among these, death curse tinctures strong enough to work on immortals. Her thoughts wandering from sacrifices to curses, Maeve came to mind. Oonagh felt a slight pang. Her father's second wife had been beautiful within and without. Having never known her own mother's love, Oonagh instantly bonded with her new stepmother. For five years, it had been just the two of them, and for those five years she happily imagined herself as lovely as Maeve, had imagined herself Maeve's *true* daughter. Then along came Orlaith with her expressive gray eyes and skin like cream. Oonagh angrily snipped a perfect rose bud in effigy.

Everyone knew wishes held power. Orlaith's death had been a secret desire since the day the infant was born. But fae didn't die like humans. They faded. For several years, she'd wished hard and watched Orlaith carefully to see if the child might fade. Instead Orlaith thrived and grew as lovely as Maeve's own reflection.

True, Maeve had never been uneven in her affections to either daughter, but Oonagh felt the difference nonetheless. How could she not? Courtiers always commented on the beauty Orlaith was growing to be. And *that* was all that mattered. Maeve would always reply how fortunate she was to have *two* lovely daughters. Oonagh's frown deepened. In all her life, only Maeve called her beautiful without prompting, unlike her oblivious father, who required constant reminding that his first born needed to see her own beauty reflected in his eyes.

To this day, a part of her wished she hadn't acted so rashly where her stepmother was concerned. Snipping away a sickly branch, she remembered the day she'd simply heard enough praise for her stepsister. If only she hadn't been afraid Maeve would shun her once Orlaith was dead. Such pain would have been unbearable. The only way to rid herself of Orlaith and not feel Maeve turn against her was to curse Maeve first. The book explained how. It seemed so perfect a plan at the time. But how could she have known that once given, there was no calling back such a curse?

Every time the accursed touched another living thing, its life force would slowly leech away. It had taken less than a week for her stepmother to die. On her deathbed, Maeve reached for her and said, "I'll always love you my beautiful Oonagh." Oonagh felt the last of her life force drawn away into her own hand. Maeve's loss was the single regret of her life. Fearing her father would learn of her part in Maeve's death, Oonagh poured him a goblet of mead and added several drops of the curse. This he drank and sealed his fate. With so many hugs of sympathy over the death of his wife, he faded away in just two days.

Oonagh scowled. The same curse had no effect on Orlaith. Oonagh had even used the entire charm tincture to ensure death would come quickly. That it didn't work only made her despise her half-sister more.

As the eldest, Oonagh naturally assumed the crown, but the loss of Maeve's love and the guilt of her death brought about a chronic unhappiness. Oonagh blamed the Ban Sidhe blood, of course, but Orlaith factored in as well. Shortly after the deaths, her stepsister had taken to staying away for days and weeks at a time. Suspicious, Oonagh had her followed and discovered Orlaith was in love with a human and carrying a bairn. Immune to the curse as her stepsister might have been, Oonagh couldn't allow such temerity to stand. It had taken precise timing to have the lover killed in the snow on the knoll above. Oonagh couldn't have anticipated his death would cause Orlaith to give birth, but she had, right beside his body, and crying out his name the entire time. The surreal scene was all very dramatic, and red. Very red.

Oonagh smiled, remembering how she'd sent the half-blood babe away, to grow as a cuckoo among the warblers. She'd ordered the hob to bring another boy to the Aos Sidhe to be raised for the tithe. Her smiled faded now. Some unseen hand had interfered with her plan in an *unacceptable* turn of events. She decided then if one soul tithed to hell brought a wish, then the second soul would surely bring another, and she'd give Orlaith's changeling's son to hell in exchange for the death of his immortal mother. Oonagh clipped another perfect blossom and ground the rose under her shoe.

The sound of throat-clearing came from the doorway. Oonagh paid it little mind until two more fading rose auras presented themselves.

Billy Blin said, "My queen, I have returned with news of the changeling."

~*~

Orlaith walked among the foxgloves. Flowers always brought her parents to mind. All these years later their death haunted her, for fae never faded before their time. Their unexpected deaths still made no sense. Finding a perfect bloom, she carefully severed the stem with a flick of her silver herb knife.

"What brings you above ground, Aunt? Does my mother know you're in the vale?" Rowan's voice came from behind her.

Orlaith closed her eyes, her teeth set on edge. She didn't hate this ginger-haired young man, she reminded herself. None of this was his doing. She simply despised what he represented. Rowan had no idea he was brought here the night her own child was ripped from her arms, and that it was he who grew to manhood before her eyes, not her son. Rising, she turned to face him. "We have discussed this before, Rowan. Where I go is no one's concern."

He chuckled. "Mother would see that differently."

Mother. Charmed as he was to believe he was a fae prince, destined to one day reign, he was ignorant of the truth of his own fate. Her heart softening with the thought, she said, "Why are you here, Rowan?"

"Mother has me searching for her hob."

"*Her* hob? Billy Blin isn't a possession. He was my mother's most cherished companion and my grandmother's companion as well. Billy has been with my family for more than nine hundred years."

"And now he belongs to Mother. *Her* servant has gone missing."

Refusing to be baited further, she said simply, "Billy likes to knit at the hearth. I suggest you try the kitchens."

"I shall, Aunt. And I'll be sure to let Mother know your whereabouts."

Orlaith watched him go, a knot of sorrow tugging at her heart. That poor stolen babe raised under the foul enchantment of *The Black Opus* had grown into an extremely disagreeable young man.

Orlaith shook her head sadly. Even if she told him the truth he wouldn't believe it. She could do nothing to alter Rowan's stars. Only love had power to change a life's course, and it took more love than he would ever find in the Aos Sidhe. Oonagh had charmed him to be singularly unpleasant and this disagreeable personality prevented him from forming friendships, therefore the possibility of love did not exist for him. And that was exactly what Oonagh wanted. Rowan was raised to be sacrificed.

Kneeling, Orlaith placed the foxglove sprig on the spot where John died and Lenox was born. She closed her eyes and sent both her love. Her ears pricked at the sound of whimpering and mumbling coming from behind the ancient yew tree's massive trunk. Drawing silently to the other side, she found Billy Blin. Blood oozed through his spindly fingers, which were pressed hard to his head. His collar and shirt front were dark with it. She knelt beside the waifish hob. "Oh dear. Billy, what happened?"

He looked up at her with red-rimmed eyes. An instant later a swirl of glitter tidied his shirt. "It's nothing, my dearest."

He attempted to rise but she stayed him with her hand. "You're still bleeding and you say this is *nothing*? Allow me to help you, Billy." Orlaith gently took his hand from his ear and saw the damage. Nothing but a hole remained. She met his eyes. "I don't need to ask who's done this to you."

Billy hung his head, remaining silent.

Orlaith focused her thoughts and into her open hand appeared a small basket of powders and herbs to heal his wound.

Seeing it, Billy's words came out in a rapid string of babble. "It's nothing my dearest, truly. It's nothing, nothing, nothing to be alarmed about." To emphasize his words, he closed his eyes, and his head was engulfed by a swirl of glittering glamour. Both ears appeared fully restored, save for the fact they sparkled.

Orlaith frowned. She said, "Stop that, Billy, please. For the love we hold for one another, you *will* allow me to tend your wound. Why did my sister do this to you?"

He didn't answer, instead he said, "I fear for you if you offer me aid."

Orlaith looked him in the eye. "My mother is gone. Your reason to stay no longer exists."

Billy's eyes filled with tears. "I miss her so."

"As do I, Billy." This poor dear friend had been looking after her family since before her mother was born, and this mistreatment was how he was repaid. She dabbed the raw flesh clean with marigold water and then coated the wound with honey balm. "You need to leave the Aos Sidhe and make a good life for yourself, perhaps a nice barn somewhere . . . "

His eyes grew round. "I cannot leave!"

"Nonsense. If my mother could see how you have been abused . . . "

He shook his head. "I'm Queen Oonagh's servant now, my dear. I'm bound to her as your mother's first daughter."

She held his head and looked him in the eye, "Dear, dear Billy, we both know this is not true, for *I* am my mother's first daughter. And the only thing that holds you is love for me. I know you stay to protect me, but my sister cannot harm me more than she already has."

He placed his spindly hands over hers. "Oh she can, dearest. She can."

"How?"

Billy looked around before whispering, "She means to find the prince and with him pay the tithe for an extra wish."

SIX

The estate business was tidy for the time being. I felt the urge to stretch my legs and let my horse graze at his leisure. On foot, I ventured into the foothills on the far side of Carterhaugh lands in search of undiscovered Scottish flora for the Pendry conservatory. It was beautiful country here, with primeval trees and standing stones erected by the ancients.

What have we here? The low-growing herb was familiar. Pyrola? I carefully removed an outer leaf and tasted it. Yes, this was the rare intermediate wintergreen. I searched the ground for a robust patch and finding one, carefully cut myself a root sample and packed it away between the layers of damp moss in my tin vasculum. Mindless in the task, I found myself knee-high in thistle and gorse. *Bloody hell.*

Surrounded on three sides, there was nothing to do but press forward as sharp-needled stickers took their toll on cloth and skin. It was almost worth the wear and tear, for on the other side of the pain-studded obstacle was a most lovely glade. I walked on and soon came to a burned-out ruin on the very edge of my lands. A glance at the substantial growth of beech and fern told me some time had passed, perhaps twenty years, judging by the size of the saplings. Beyond the outer shell of this once-impressive home, I came upon a rose garden gone wild.

Tucked here and there grew the occasional late bloom the like I'd never seen before. Careful cross-pollination with Pendry roses would bring about spectacular blooms. The thought had me on my knees searching for the healthiest root stock to bring home. That thought evaporated, however, when I heard a woman singing.

The lovely sound drew nearer and I stayed on my knees, lest my appearance startle the woman and end the song. When I peered through the shrubbery, I couldn't believe my eyes. Here was Selene the moon goddess come to earth, and she had taken the form of Janet Roxburgh. She moved among the weeds, plucking this and that for her basket. My heart started to pound and longing swept over me. Fighting the urge to rise then and there, I used my hidden vantage to drink her in. What an ethereal beauty she was, with those fair tresses tucked up under her straw hat. She'd climbed through the thicket as I had and her fair cheeks were painted with a blush of exertion. The witch was lovely.

She straightened suddenly and turned to look in my direction. I hadn't made a sound, and concealed as I was, and I wondered if she'd sensed me hiding there. Her words confirmed it.

"Show yourself."

Caught as a Peeping Tom, I could do naught but stand and present myself.

She took a wary step backward. Though her eyes appeared fearful, I noticed the glint of a silver herb knife clutched tightly in her hand. This she pointed at me when she addressed me angrily. "What are you about, sir?"

Her flashing eyes were such a vivid hue they gave me pause. They were the color of violets in springtime. "Hello, allow me to introduce myself, I'm the new —"

"— I don't care *what* you are," she interrupted, her words tinged with ire, "I want to know *who* you are, sir, to be hiding in the brush watching me?"

Taken aback by the woman's sharp tongue and an attitude that didn't mesh with my dream of her, I found my voice. Tipping my head to the basket in her hand, I said with a little prickle of my own, "And who are *you*, Miss, to be on *my* lands helping yourself to *my* herbs?"

Those violet eyes suddenly grew wide and then narrowed just as fast. I thought she'd speak, but instead gave me her defiant chin. In the next instant, she spun on her heel and ran off.

Stunned, I could only blink. I contemplated running after her but thrown off-kilter by this poor meeting, I thought otherwise. Instead, I gathered my gear and returned to Carterhaugh.

A cold drenching rain began to fall the instant I entered the stable. The stable lad rushed to take my horse, and a footman named Barney met me with opened umbrella. Taking my gear, he said, "Did ye enjoy yer outing, yer lairdship?"

"I did, Barney. See my equipment into the library, if you would."

"Aye, sir."

We rushed along the walkway and he saw me inside a good deal dryer than he was. Munro waited to close the door behind us just as the sky broke open in a downpour. He said, "Oh it's a good thing ye made it back before the storm grew worse, yer lairdship. I've instructed a hot bath be ready fer ye, just in case."

"That sounds excellent, Munro."

"Might I tempt ye with hot tea, sir? Or would ye prefer whiskey? His auld lairdship always took a nip after his outings. Though more for his rheumatism than pleasure, I'm sure."

After my confounding encounter with the witch, a whiskey sounded superb. "Excellent idea, Munro. Do send it up."

"As ye wish, yer lairdship."

Alone in my bath, I sipped my scotch and replayed the exchange with Janet Roxburgh. Her demeanor toward me was in sharp contrast to the friendly woman I'd seen at MacPhee's Peg. My earlier conversation with Mrs. Frew provided insight. MacPhee's mother disdained a healer, no, a *witch*, helping her grandchildren into the world. If Grannie MacPhee took issue, did others as well?

As a boy I'd discovered my perception was keener than most. It rarely steered me wrong. I opened my mind to it now and my intuition told me Janet had cause to be wary. I'd popped out like a hedgehog and startled her. Her resultant fear was a natural occurrence, as was the supposed anger she flashed to cover the fact. Thinking on it now, the badger came to mind. A cornered badger would feint an attack to frighten potential foes away.

Setting my glass aside, I closed my eyes and sank into the water. I saw her in my mind's eye as she walked from sunlight to shade and back, her lovely hair framing her face in damp ringlets. I imagined that the pink tint so pretty upon her cheeks lay elsewhere too. Suddenly her beautiful violet eyes flashed daggers at me, causing my wanton daydream to pop like a soap bubble. "Damn," I chuckled. "Witch or not, you've certainly cast your spell upon me."

Potts poked his head around the corner and I sat forward. No need to startle the poor fellow.

His eyes traveled the room before asking, "I'm sorry, sir, I didn't fully hear . . . "

Reaching for my glass, I raised it to him, "Talking to my scotch is all."

He chuckled. "Ah. I thought you'd want to know, sir. There's a letter come for you."

"From my mother, is it?" I couldn't imagine why she'd write so soon. Perhaps the greenhouse succumbed to aphids after all.

Potts nodded. "I don't believe so, sir. I was in the kitchen when it arrived. A lad brought it from the town. Mr. Munro is holding the letter for you.

A few minutes later, I made my way down the stairs, and found Munro waiting for me.

"This arrived fer ye, yer lairdship," he said.

I thanked him and read an invitation for dinner a week from Saturday addressed by Eppa the headmaster, the man Mrs. Frew declared "worth my trouble to meet." I handed the letter back to Munro, and said, "Please send Mr. Eppa my reply. Thank him for his invitation, and tell him I shall look forward to our dinner engagement."

I saw a brief glimmer of surprise on the butler's face. His bland mask returning, he replied with a nod. "Verra good, sir."

Was I so very different from these Scots that my every action brought about a look of surprise? Centuries ago, England had done wrong by these people. Was this the source of their reaction, that they expected the same from me and showed surprise when I didn't deliver to that long conceived notion? Innkeeper MacPhee's words came back to me: *I canna say it'll be easy fer an outlander to find himself at Carterhaugh.*

It wasn't difficult in the least. Just odd.

SEVEN

Better than a week passed since chancing upon Janet at the Roxburgh ruins. Thoughts of her weren't relegated to daydreams between sorting out the estate, for the lovely witch filled my nights as well. Finishing my accounts, I gathered my gear and set out for the abandoned rose garden hoping for another chance encounter.

The morning's cold rains inspired a slow-rising fog that met the sun with an uncomfortably cloying humidity. By the time I'd climbed the gorse and thistle hillside, I was drenched with sweat. By midday, I determine my elusive witch wasn't going to show herself.

It was hellishly warm for this time of the year and the stream just beyond the thicket looked splendidly refreshing. My coat and waistcoat long discarded, I rolled up my sleeves and fashioned myself a walking stick to aid my footing down the slope. Nearing the bend, I heard voices from the other side of a large downed willow. The conversation stopped me in my tracks.

A husky voice whispered, "By god, look a' her. No! Don't ye look. I'll tell ye. She has skin like fresh cream, she has. Now remember what we talked about, Georgie? Yer t' cover her face an' hold her down while I gi' her a poke. I dinna want her t' see it's me, aye?"

Another voice, presumably Georgie's, said, "Tha's no verra fair to me, Arch, t' watch ye have yer way."

"Ye *won't* watch! Ye know I've wanted tha' lass fer meself me whole life. After today, she'll be spoiled. Her father will welcome me t' take her."

Another voice spoke up. "An' what will *I* do, Arch? Arch? Did ye hear what I asked ye, what'll *I* do?"

Arch growled his warning, "Shh! She'll hear ye, ye bloody half-brained bugger."

Lowering his voice, the man asked, "But what d' ye want us to do after we put the sack on her?"

Arch hissed, "Ye hold her down an' farkin' close yer eyes and keep yer mouth shut! Janet Roxburgh will be me wife Georgie, an' dinna *you* an' Willie ever forget it. No matter wha' ye hear today."

I couldn't believe my ears. *Bloody bastards!* They were bent upon rape to force Janet into marriage. Rage consumed me. It was all I could do to not vault over the trunk and soundly thrash the three with my walking stick. Every outcome played in my mind at once. If I confronted them, it was three against one and I could be rendered useless to protect her. An idea struck me. I hurried through the woods to the far side of the stream, all the while watching for the miscreants to show themselves.

Unprepared for the vision, I felt my chest constrict at the sight of a naiad at her bath. Janet bathed in naked abandon, unaware of the vipers hiding near. I quickly undressed and then silently waded in her direction. Near enough to be heard by the villains, I loudly called, "Janet darling, go to the deeper water. Those men by the felled willow might be overcome by my wife's beauty. I know I certainly am."

Whirling first to me, then to the men I'd outed, Janet immediately immersed herself.

I heard a growl of outrage from the vicinity of the tree. "Wife! Bloody farkin' hell. I'm *done* w' this *faithless* bitch. Are ye buggers comin' or no?"

The two men jogged after him, both pleading, "Hold up, Arch!"

I watched to be sure they'd left the glen, and then turned back to see Janet submerged to her chin. I assured her, "They're gone."

She rose from the water like Aphrodite.

My eyes longed to remain on this vision, but the gentleman I was born and bred to be came to the fore and I gave her my back. I explained that I'd overheard a foul plot to see her compromised and expressed my regret for any discomfort I might have caused her, adding, "I was outnumbered, I'm afraid."

Splashing told me she was making her way toward the bank. When she spoke, her words were a distance away. "Thank you. Archie MacGilliveray has finally shown his true colors, as I knew he would one day."

I stole a glance toward the bank where Janet was dressing. Wading there, I continued, "That man now believes you are my wife and have been spoken for. He's sure to leave you alone. He had it in his mind you'd marry him after today." With her back to me, I hastily donned my clothes.

"He declared himself last month, and didn't take my refusal well."

Understanding filled me. This was the reason for her sharp demeanor the day before. More statement than question, I said, "He's trailed you before."

She turned to me and nodded. "Archie and his friends have followed me everywhere for years. I had no idea he'd try something like this. I am forever grateful, Mr — ?"

"Lenox," I said and held my hand out to her. "And you are?"

"Janet." She took my hand. Unbelievably, I felt a tingle all the way up my arm. The sensation was extraordinary. I wanted more. That her violet eyes grew large had me wondering whether she felt it as well.

Bemused by her look of surprise, I lingered over her fingers until she eased her hand from mine. I didn't want her to go. I wanted to see if that tingle could also be felt at her lips. I believed the answer was yes. I wondered what it might feel like to chase that tingle over her body. Hoping she'd linger, I caught her hand again. "Must you leave?"

Her gaze went to our hands then came back to my eyes. I saw confusion in those violet depths.

She said, "Yes. I must be getting back." Again she slipped her hand from mine. A smile played upon her lips. That was all. She turned and hurried off.

I watched her go and squelched the urge to run after her. In all likelihood, she was unsettled over the events at the stream. I pondered that. Other women of my acquaintance would have been reduced to tears, or quite possibly, hysterics over such a thing. Not Miss Janet Roxburgh. Here was a strong, beautiful, accomplished woman. And I, the besotted fool, was in love.

~*~

Orlaith watched the moon and waited. The weather was changing and a storm was coming in with the clouds. When the celestial orb slipped behind cloud cover, she moved quickly, lest the shadow end and catch her in the open. It was a risk to come, but there was no choice in the matter. Not after Billy confided that Oonagh planned to murder Lenox. The sky cleared again. She ducked beside the hedge and waited for darkness.

With Eppa and Billy gone, trusted friends were few. She had many friends among the court, but they were afraid, and rightfully so. Though she knew they would help her if she asked, she wouldn't involve them. The savagery done to poor Billy stuck like a thick lump of emotion in her throat. Never again would anyone be hurt on her behalf. She was alone in this.

What had caused her sister to become so cruel? Their parents raised them the same, loved them the same. There was no reason she could fathom, unless this was an issue of blood. Oonagh's true mother had been half Ban Sidhe, and those beings were known to set their minds on a single course, often deep melancholia. Again the clouds covered the moon. Thoughts in turmoil, she hurried across the open field.

~*~

Amelia Pendry was awake when the hall clock struck eleven times. In fact, she hadn't slept a wink. She snapped her locket closed and put it in her pocket for safekeeping. Stepping over the snoring Dudley, she tiptoed down the stairs. The last thing she needed was to wake the house. Though she trusted Fanny and Osgood implicitly, she wouldn't involve the servants in this. How could she ever explain it without admitting the truth of her son? She gently closed the library door behind her and lit a lamp.

That morning, a linnet had flown down the chimney. Right before her disbelieving eyes, the bird had changed itself into a note that fluttered and landed at the foot of her bed. Taking it from her pocket now, she held it near the lamp and read it again.

Dearest Lady Pendry,

I promised myself I would not contact you again, however, the situation has changed and we must speak. Please meet me in the end stall of your stable at half past midnight tonight.

Yours,
Orlaith

Tucking it away, she exited quietly through the library doors.

~*~

Orlaith entered the dark stable and was met with the night sound of horses and the light snoring of two stablemen in the loft above. No other could hear the conversation she was about to have, so she focused her thoughts and sent a gift of supreme comfort to the occupants of the loft. The snoring ceased. The stablemen would sleep soundly until dawn.

She heard the careful sound of the latch turning. There was no need to ask Amelia if she'd come alone, her mother's heart would guide her.

Amelia whispered, "Orlaith, are you here?"

"I am."

Amelia followed the voice to the last stall and ducked inside. Lit by intermitted moonlight, Orlaith held her arms out, and said, "We meet at last, Lady Amelia."

The two mothers hugged. Amelia, startled, drew back. "Lenox feels as you do, when you touch him. This, this . . . *tingling.*" Apparently at a loss for words, Amelia shook her head. Then she said, "Is this sensation particular to all fae?

"It is." Orlaith nodded in the darkness. She briefly explained, "We are a different people, Amelia, for all our similarities. Compare mine to all of nature rather than your own kind." She felt Amelia's curiosity, and she had questions of her own. But there was no time to ask.

"How — "

Interrupting, Orlaith put her hand up. "Forgive me, Amelia. I must tell you I have very little time. It is urgent that I say what it is I've come to say."

"Of course. Why have you come?"

"I'd planned to leave you and Lenox to each other's care, for I only knew him as he grew inside me and only for a moment at his birth, before he was ripped from my arms. Circumstance made you a truer mother to him than I." Her voice cracked and she turned away to compose herself.

Amelia placed a comforting hand upon her back. "All of my children died the day they were born. I understand. If it may bring any softening to your pain at all, know I have loved him honestly, as his true mother would."

Turning back, Orlaith smiled softly. "I know this. And I love you for it." She went on to explain about their son's father.

Amelia put her hands to her mouth. Wide-eyed she whispered, "*John*? My husband's brother John is Lenox's father?"

Orlaith nodded. "We met in the ancient grove and fell in love. He was coming to take me away when my sister found us. She killed him. So distraught was I, my son was born there, right beside his father's body. The babe was taken away and there was nothing I could do."

"How *terrible*. Oh poor, poor, John. I didn't know how Lenox came to me that night. I had just given birth, but I knew . . . " Amelia wiped her eyes. "I knew he wasn't mine. I lost my Evan not two weeks before, you see. I, I knew the baby was a, a — "

"— changeling," Orlaith offered.

"Yes." Amelia went silent for a short time, then pulled a letter from her pocket and handed it over. "What does this mean?"

Orlaith read:

My Dear Lady Pendry,

We ride on December 31st and he will return with us.

Queen Oonagh

"It means the queen intends to sacrifice Lenox in an ancient *tithe to hell*," Orlaith said.

Amelia blinked. "*What?* But that's — that's a *faerie* story!"

"Faery story it may be, in your world, but it was once an ancient practice in mine."

"Forgive my ignorance Orlaith, but I don't understand this. What purpose could killing my son . . . *our* son, have? What does this barbarism serve?"

"If there *is* a purpose, I don't know it, other than my sister wishes to cause me more pain."

"Your *sister?*"

Orlaith nodded. "Oonagh was born to our father's first wife."

"Then he is her *blood*, her *nephew!*" Amelia said.

Orlaith could see the fear and questions burning in the woman's eyes, but she had no answers to give. "As I've said, her reason for any of this has yet to be revealed to me. I do know this, she is furious to find Lenox gone."

Amelia gasped. Her hands flew to her mouth to silence the sound. Hushed words came through her fingers, "She knows he's in Selkirk?"

"I am not certain what she knows." Orlaith shook her head. "But he must stay away from here, Amelia, at least until his birthday. I've read the ancient legends. The tithe was very specific. The offering must be twenty-four years old on the final stroke of midnight. Only as the wheel of the year turns will blood be spilled."

Amelia grew quiet a moment, and then said, "He plans to return for his birthday." She squared her shoulders. "I shall assure him he's needed there. If that fails, I'll go to him instead."

Taking the woman's hands, Orlaith told her, "Yes, do *anything* to keep him away." Thunder rumbled in the distance. "I must go."

"Wait, I have something for you," Amelia said, pulling the locket from the folds of her gown and handing it over. "There are two photographs — one taken when Lenox was just three years of age, and the other was taken earlier this year."

Orlaith took the locket and closed her other hand into a fist. When she opened it again, a small glowing orb floated above her palm. This she released into the air and it hovered above, casting a soft light. Amelia stared wide-eyed. The horse in the next stall nickered calmly.

Orlaith opened the locket and looked at the face she'd only imagined these last twenty-four years. Her eyes misted. "Oh, how he looks like his father. He could be John's own fetch." She swallowed hard and her tears fell freely. "Thank you Amelia, *thank you* from the bottom of my heart."

Amelia wiped her own emotion away. "I've often wondered why I saw both Evan and John's reflection in Lenox. I thought it merely wishful thinking on my part." She added softly, "John was a good man and a dear brother. Evan and I both loved him deeply. Both of them would be proud of Lenox. He is everything they were in life, and more."

"Then he is the best of men," Orlaith said, putting the gold chain around her neck. She tucked the locket next to her heart.

Amelia hugged her close. "The very best."

EIGHT

Nearly two weeks had passed since I had thwarted the bounders who intended to ravish Janet. Every morning, I checked on Mrs. Frew and then took myself to the glade and stream bank that I might see my fair witch again, but each visit found her absent. I couldn't get Janet out of my waking thoughts, nor did I want to. Every detail had been burned into my mind. Even in my dreams did I wade into that stream, drawn to her splendor. But in those dreams, she came to me. I held the water nymph in my arms and kissed her sweet lips and filled my hands with her softness. My last dream had progressed well beyond my imagined kisses. I woke in such a state, for an instant I wondered if the dream incident actually occurred.

~*~

Declining the carriage for my journey to Headmaster Eppa's home, I had one of the young Ennis boys saddle a horse.

The town below the manse was friendly and busy, and I was treated to more than one tipped hat and curtsey that included a perplexing assortment of "Ye couldn't do better, yer lairdship." I spied young Penny MacPhee jostling her squalling infant brother on her shoulder while her mother haggled with a peddler over his too-green pears. Adjusting the bundle in her arms, Penny treated me to a bright smile before hushing her brother with a fingertip to suck on. I tipped my hat to the lot. "Good day, ladies."

Mrs. MacPhee and the peddler said in tandem, "G'day yer lairdship!"

I asked, "Might you direct me to the schoolmaster's residence?"

Both women looked completely confused by my question. The grinning peddler said, "Yer destination is nigh a quarter mile at th' end o' Grant's Road afore ye come t' th' bridge, on th' left. Ye'll see th' bell at th' door, no missin' it. Master Eppa lives in th' wee stone cottage behind th' school."

I nodded. "And Grant's Road is . . . ?"

She pointed over my shoulder to MacPhee's Peg. "Ye must turn left at th' peg."

I thanked them for this odd exchange, and heading there, soon found myself at the schoolhouse gate and then the small cottage behind. The door opened and a tall handsome fellow of indeterminate age emerged. I tipped my hat, "Headmaster Eppa, I presume?"

He met me with an expression of pure astonishment, then suddenly broke into a wide welcoming smile. "Lord of All! Yes, I am he, and you must be *Laird Carter*."

I chuckled. "Laird I may be, but a Carter only on my mother's side. Lenox Pendry, late of London, at your service, sir."

His eyes sparkled. "Do come in, son. Tell me how it is you've come to be in this distant place."

I followed him inside. Such a light and airy space I'd never have guessed from the austere facade. "I'm told you knew my uncle, Master Eppa."

He took my hat and gloves. "Eppa, please. And yes, I did. A fine man, Charles Carter. Excuse me." He left and returned a moment later with a slight-framed youth in tow. The headmaster said, "Billy, please see Master Lenox Pendry's horse paddocked and relieved of his saddle."

Catching sight of me, the youth's eyes grew wide and his head whipped to the headmaster, who simply smiled and nodded. What the devil was it with these Scots? I was beginning to suspect I had a second head growing out of my shoulders visible only to Scotsmen.

Billy said, "Right away, yes sir, yes sir, yes sir, I'll see to the young pri–, the young *master's* horse."

I watched the odd young fellow go and for an instant it appeared the boy didn't have ears and in that hallucination it appeared he wasn't a boy all, but a spindly-limbed, well, a spindly-limbed *what* I couldn't say. I rubbed the mirage from my eyes.

A note of unaccountable happiness laced Master Eppa's tone when he said, "Billy is a fine cook. I hope you're not averse to rarebit. We are not meat eaters, you see."

~*~

The young prince, is here! Billy couldn't believe his eyes. Orlaith's son all grown. Somehow the last image of the boy, at age six, had stuck with him. He reached into his trouser pocket and a handkerchief that wasn't there a moment ago materialized in his hand. He dabbed his eyes then blew his nose; the honking sound made the horse blow and stomp his foot.

Patting the animal, he whispered, "No, I'm *not* sad, but thank you for your concern, my dear. I'm very happy! Mine are tears of joy." Billy gave the horse a scoop of oats. The horse whinnied and swept his long tail from side to side. The hob shook his head and told him, "*No*, you *can't* have *more*. Too much will bind you up!" He tipped his head to the pasture. "You'll find good grass at the far end of the field, now go."

Turning back to the kitchen, an idea suddenly struck him. Billy whistled and a snow bunting flew to the currant bush beside the porch stairs. Checking first to be sure he was alone, he once again reached into his trouser pocket and this time pulled out a small rolled tube of paper. This too wasn't there a moment ago. He unrolled and it and whispered the text he wished upon it, the words sparkling as they came into being. He rolled it up again and held out a finger for the bird to perch upon. Speaking softly, for bird alone, he said, "My dear, I have a message for you to deliver. Not everything I wish to say can be said in here. You must remember the rest for me."

The bird gripped the message in his little claw and listened as Billy whispered in his ear. Message complete, he flew off.

"What are you up to, Billy?"

Startled, Billy jumped. "Oh! Janet, it's you."

Janet smiled at her father's oldest friend who recently had come to live with them. She said, "I've been harvesting mushrooms all afternoon. Why are you the boy today?"

"Your father has company . . . someone who may not wish to see an old crone with his dinner."

She didn't long ponder his odd explanation, for she blurted, "I *completely* forgot father's dinner guest comes today. Oh look at me, Billy. I'm not fit for company." She ran a dirty hand down her apron.

Billy focused his mind on the upstairs window. Immediately a sparkling staircase leading up to a sparkling door appeared along the outside wall.

"Billy!" Janet spun around to be sure no one saw the hob's magic. She whirled back and whispered, "Someone might see."

He took her hand and patted it. Shaking his head, he assured her, "It's our kind who sees the reality of the glamour, Janet. To the rest, it's only a trick of light."

"I am sorry, Billy. I didn't mean to be abrupt. There are those who treat me with suspicion for simply using herbs to heal. I can only imagine how they'd feel about your skills, let alone the truth of you. Fear of the unknown causes people who normally think clearly to lose their senses. I couldn't bear it if someone hurt you. It's hard to be different sometimes."

He nodded. "This is not our world, Janet, no matter the best of it we make for ourselves. Now off off off with you, dear girl, go to your room where a hot bath waits. Your father entertains his guest alone."

Janet kissed the top of his head. "I'm glad you're here with us, Billy. It's only been a short while, but I feel as though you've always been in my life. Thank you for the bath, and my stairs." With that, she hurried up the stairway. The instant she closed the magic door behind her, the whole structure briefly glittered then was gone.

Billy headed to the kitchen but stopped midway. The young prince was here and a message in flight to Orlaith. Finally one great wrong could be made right. The other wrong still sat heavy in his heart. He took a deep breath and let it out slowly. What he was about to do came with a price.

He plucked a leaf from the ash tree at the fence and ducked around to the side of the house. Holding the small leaf tucked between his palms he spoke to it. Color drained from body, starting at the crown of his head. It coursed down his arms and filled his hands until the leaf sparkled. This siphoning done, he drew a tired breath and whistled. A nearby nightingale answered. The bird landed on top of his head then hopped to the finger he offered.

The nightingale eyed him up and down then chittered softly.

Billy reassured her. "Don't fret my dear. I appreciate your concern, but I'm only a bit tired from this magic. I have a very important task, if you would help me."

The small bird bobbed her head up and down several times.

Billy smiled. "And to thank you I will save crumbs for your return. You are to fly to the Aos Sidhe and wait for the ginger-haired changeling. You will know him. He is the only one there." Billy held the sparkling leaf out to the nightingale, who grasped it in his foot. Billy explained the important task, then watched the bird fly away. He'd recently come to the conclusion that in order to dissolve the powerful charm of *The Black Opus* he must give of his own life essence. His kind lived extremely long lives. To lose one year, ten, or even one hundred was the least he could do to make amends to Rowan the changeling.

~*~

Master Eppa handed me a horn cup. I took a sip and tasted wine of some sort, one I couldn't readily identify. I said, "Your wine is quite good. I admit I can't place the flavor."

"You've never had mead then?"

"Ah, *mead*. I've heard of it, yes, but not tasted it until this moment." I raised my cup to him. "Very good, sir. It's *very* good."

"My daughter will be glad to hear it. She makes our wine."

I nodded my appreciation. The flavor was subtle and now that I knew, I could taste the floral undertone of the honey.

"So laird Carter, may call you by your given name?"

"Please."

"Lenox, I am a curious man. Pray tell, how does an Englishman of your rank find his way to this small corner of the earth?"

"My mother was eager to see me handle the estate of her late uncle, Charles."

He raised his glass slightly in acknowledgment of his friend's passing. "To Charlie. I very much miss him."

I followed suit. "I hear he was quite the generous fellow." A delicious aroma wafted from the far end of the cottage and I could hear sounds of dishes and pots rattling. My stomach rumbled.

"Charlie was the heart and soul of generosity, a fine man and a dear friend at a time when I found myself alone in the world." He refilled our glasses. "So tell me about you, Lenox. What are your interests, son?"

Master Eppa and I chatted about my life at Pendry. Here I'd just met the man, yet felt a comfortable compatibility one normally gained over a lifetime. He seemed intent to know every detail of my life there, as though he was assembling a puzzle and each bit gained him a new piece. It was curious.

Suddenly, he looked over my shoulder and his face broke into a wide smile. He said, "I was wondering when we'd see you. Lenox, may I present my Janet, the light of my life."

Hoping his Janet was one and the same as *my* Janet, I jumped to my feet and turned. The act caused my chair to fall backward and scatter a basket filled with balls of yarn and knitting needles. She rushed forward just as I bent to retrieve the rolling balls and the two of us solidly butted heads.

"Ow!" we exclaimed at once and rose, laughing. I hurried my apology and set the chair to rights.

She rubbed the crown of her head and laughingly told me, "Goodness, you've such a hard head!"

Gathering yarn from a ball that had made it across the room, her father

69

chuckled over my comedy of errors. He added, "As I was saying, this outspoken sprite is my daughter Janet. Janet, dear, allow me to introduce you to Lenox Pendry, the new Laird of Carterhaugh, Laird Charlie's nephew."

I held my hand to her. "I'm pleased to make your acquaintance, Janet."

She gave me a look that was clearly tinged with mirth. "As am I, your *lairdship.*"

The mocking emphasis on my title took her father by surprise, for he turned to her, then back to me, he said, "I sense the two of you have already met."

I nodded. "I had the pleasure of meeting your daughter in a rose garden beside the ruins of a manor house."

Master Eppa tsked, "*Janet . . .*"

"Papa, I was *fine*. Where else would I find the foxglove needed for Mrs. Frew's tincture?"

"I've deemed it unsafe for you to venture there on your own," he said. "Archie MacGilliveray is not one to take no for an answer."

I felt like I'd just stepped in manure with my best shoes. Clearly I'd unintentionally given her secret away. Turning away from this father–daughter discussion in a feeble attempt to give them privacy, I set the knitting basket to rights and noticed the lad Billy in the doorway. He was smiling at me from ear to ear as if I were some long lost relation. I was struck with the notion there was more to the boy than anyone knew. What a peculiar young fellow.

Janet said, "You'll be pleased to know, Papa, that Lenox put to sleep, once and for all, all hopes Archie MacGilliveray had that I'd marry him." She went to my side and threaded her arm through mine. The electric tingle was felt all the way to my toes and my besotted heart began to pound. She added, "Lenox made it quite clear that he was to leave me alone."

What she expected by that statement I can't say, but I expected a father's condemnation of such a stunt. Such an intimate declaration would certainly taint his daughter's reputation if word of it spread. What I got instead was a thigh-slapping hoot. His words fizzing with joy, he said to Billy in the doorway, "Billy, did you hear? Lenox is my daughter's champion!"

"Yes yes yes, I heard!" Like a small child learning the puppet show was coming to town, the lad hopped up and down. For a second, the look of him altered and I could swear he looked like he'd walked off the pages of one of the fairy books Osgood collected. He had a largish earless head, beaky nose, and spindly limbs and in no way looked like the boy I knew him to be. I blinked and looked again. No, just an exuberant boy. I eyed my cup of mead warily and set it on the table. Perhaps the drink was stronger than I knew.

The headmaster asked, "And how was this accomplished?"

Smiling, Janet said, "Lenox told Archie he and I were *secretly* man and wife. The entire village surely knows by now."

The smile instantly vanished from her father's face.

I felt Janet stiffen beside me. She hurried to explain.

The explanation didn't make it more palatable. In fact, the words hit me squarely between the eyes. In that moment, I heard what a father would hear.

Sure enough, Eppa said, "Have you no care for your reputation, Janet? This is your *home*. There are townspeople here who see your healing arts as questionable. Were you to add a false declaration of marriage — to the Laird of Carterhaugh no less . . . ." He shook his head.

Her tight-lipped scowl said it all. I could almost picture the argument forming in the storm cloud over her head. She dropped my arm and protested, "Papa, Lenox was simply coming to my aid when the ruse was made . . . He and I, we — " She turned to me hopelessly.

I finished, "Sir, I assure you. Your daughter and I have nothing between us other than that moment where, with a few poorly chosen words, I averted a plot by Mr. MacGilliveray."

He drew a long breath and let it out slowly. To me he said, "Do *you* not see the dilemma, Lenox?"

I did. I also saw the answer to my dreams. I said, "Your father is absolutely correct, Janet. At the time, I saw no other way to stop Archie's foul intentions." I explained the odds were three against one and what my ultimate worry was. Catching his slight nod of approval, I told the headmaster sincerely, "I deeply apologize for compromising your daughter, sir, and for bringing this potential ruin upon your good name. I would offer to make my ruse a reality." I met his eye briefly and then I held my hand to her. I said, "Janet Roxburgh, would you do me the honor, that is, may I ask for your hand in marriage?"

Eyeing my hand like it were a venomous viper, she answered my proposal with a resounding, "No!" With that, she turned on her heel and ran up the stairs.

Reeling from her abrupt refusal, I felt a solid ache in my chest and recognized it for what it was, the ache of unrequited love. I'd never been in love before, not like this. Feeling a crush of sadness, I needed my own solitude in that awkward moment. Turning to my host, I said, "I'll take my leave, sir. Again, my sincere apologies."

Singularly unfazed, Master Eppa shook his head. "Nonsense. We've yet to have our dinner, and I'm certain it's ready, isn't it Billy?"

The lad wiped his tears on his cuff and nodded. He looked at me with sad eyes, then hurried into the kitchen, where I heard his not-so-quiet sobbing amid the clatter of china. I felt the same.

Master Eppa explained, "Our Billy is a sensitive soul. Come, this will all sort itself out in time, son."

My chance for escaping this uncomfortable situation disappeared when he put an arm around my shoulders and led me to the table. I was immediately engulfed by a surge of tingling power, of the like I'd only read about in the electricity experiments publicly performed by Nikola Tesla.

Billy had prepared for us an incomparable meal the likes of which I had never tasted. I sensed a silent communication between Janet's father and Billy, for the lad ate quickly and then excused himself to sit by the fire with his knitting. Janet remained cloistered in her room for the evening, but the headmaster shared a wealth of information on his life since coming here, though he never once said from whence he hailed. I delicately explained the mishap at the river without the added details of our nude bathing. Lenient father though he may be, were I him, I'd find *that* well beyond my tolerance.

He went on to explain Janet and the world she grew up in. Coming to Archie MacGilliveray, he detailed the miscreant's relentless pursuit these last few years. When Janet formally refused the man's offer of marriage several months past, Archie grew angry. The headmaster demanded he leave his daughter alone or the authorities would be contacted. Apparently Archie saw her compromise as the sure bet. *The bloody bounder.*

Through the course of conversation, I learned the history of the Roxburgh ruins and the abandoned rose garden that were now a part of the Carter lands. I now understood what spurred his earlier disapproval. It was his concern that Archie MacGilliveray might find Janet alone there with no one to come to her aid. He thanked me. I assured him I hadn't seen hide nor hair of the man on my outings.

To my surprise, he was very interested in my botanical pursuits. We talked of flowers for a time and I discovered he had a most amazing understanding of horticulture. With a father's pride, he told me how his daughter's knowledge surpassed his. I mentioned I was grateful for Janet's expert handing of my housekeeper's health. That door open, he described for me in detail just how special she was. Before long, I realized I was purposely being given detailed insight into the willful beauty who had so vehemently rebutted my proposal. I had the distinct impression my host felt his daughter would come around to the idea of being my wife. But she had vehemently refused my offer. I'd not have him press the issue upon her.

There was no doubt Janet Roxburgh had plucked my heartstrings the moment I saw her descend the tavern stairs. But my optimism had flown when faced with the truth, for I'd seen the look in her eye. My longing for the moonlit witch was a completely one-sided affair.

From start to finish, my evening was unlike what one expects to find taking dinner with a lowlands schoolmaster. I rode home to Carterhaugh feeling wholly disconcerted. What's more, I had an ache just under my breastbone. Had it been physically possible, I'd swear my heart was broken in two.

Back on Grant's Road and led by the promise of diversion, I ventured to MacPhee's Peg.

NINE

Eppa balanced a tray in one hand and knocked on his daughter's door. "May I come in? I've brought you something to eat."

"Come in Papa, but I don't care to talk about what occurred earlier."

Closing the door behind him, he set the tray on the bedside table and took a seat at the end of her bed. He watched her pounce on the meal and chuckled. "I thought you might be hungry. You should have dined with us."

She swallowed quickly and opened her mouth to speak but he stayed her with a raised hand and said, "You *may* not care to discuss this, but we *will.* Your behavior tonight was disappointing. It caused our guest embarrassment and it embarrassed me as well. Beyond that, it caused Billy sadness. And that dear fellow has had far more than his share."

"But Papa — "

"No." He shook his head. "There is no excuse for such unacceptable behavior by the lady of this house." He waited for her to absorb his words and she did.

"Yes, you're right. I *did* behave badly. I'm very sorry."

Eppa tucked a pale blonde lock of hair behind his daughter's slightly pointed ear. Side-stepping the issue momentarily, they chatted about the day. Seeing an opportunity to discuss her first meeting with Lenox, he asked leading questions and before long had a better picture of just what transpired at the river. The young man's omission of details was meant to protect her. Lenox's human inclination to protect her modesty undoubtedly came from the environment he was raised in.

Eppa said, "It won't be long before the village hears the rumor of your secret marriage and it won't matter if the tale is true or not. Your reputation will be marred —"

"— I don't care," she cut in. "I never care what people say."

That wasn't true. More than once did this precious child cry herself to sleep because of callous remarks made by people suspicious of the auld ways. And some condemned her for the fact that her parents never married.

"*I* care, Janet. This criticism will not come as a stray comment about your healing skills. From Lenox's description of the event at the stream, I think it likely Archie will cast aspersions on your character or share the news that you are wed to Lenox. Rumor will mark you in two ways."

"I don't understand."

He looked her in the eye. "The first marks you as the Lady of Carterhaugh with the title and respect that is your birthright. Your mother was such a lady. This is the life she wished for you — a life *I* cannot give. Should you dismiss Lenox's proposal, you'll be considered a woman of loose moral fiber who, at the least, bathes with a man who is not her husband."

Her eyes grew large then quickly misted. Apparently this was something she hadn't considered. "But Archie . . . was going to, to — ," she swallowed hard. "That is, he planned . . . " The tears fell.

He took her hands in his, and said softly, "I recognize Lenox as a man of character. Do you not see what he has offered by coming to your aid then and now? Can you not see his genuine feeling for you?"

She shook her head slightly. "How can he have *genuine* feelings? We don't know one another, Papa."

Sensing Janet wished to believe Lenox's feelings were true, he made a decision. "You know what we are, what I am. You know where Billy and I come from."

"Yes Papa, I know we are different from everyone here. You are fae, I am half fae, and Billy is a hob. You both come from the under hill of the Aos Sidhe."

A gentle smile played upon Eppa's lips. Janet knew the words only. To keep her safe from Oonagh, he had never shared more than that bit. Janet had never known the magic of the Aos Sidhe nor the majesty of the oak orchard that grew from acorns rooted in the time before time. She had never known her own kind. He said, "You're old enough. It's high time you knew more."

She looked at him expectantly.

"Many years ago when I was little more than a boy, I fell in love with a special girl — "

Janet smiled and interrupted, "Mama."

Eppa shook his head. "I loved your mother true. Annabel gave me reason to live when I had none. But no, it was long ago when my whole world was the Aos Sidhe and the lands above. More than eighty years have passed loving Orlaith from afar. And in all those years I loved her to the depth of my soul. I love her still."

"Didn't you tell her?"

"Her standing in the Aos Sidhe dictated I seek permission from her father before making my feelings known to her. The day I'd planned to ask his permission to court his daughter, his wife died suddenly and his death came shortly after. It was then the eldest daughter became the head of the family. As she had made her affections known to me, a sentiment I did not return, my request to wed her sister was denied. I was told if I mentioned my feelings in her presence again, I would be put to death and Orlaith would wish she'd followed me to the grave."

Janet frowned. "How hateful. What did you do?"

"I kept my feelings to myself to protect her. Orlaith was vulnerable there. Her sister was slipping into madness."

"Who was this madwoman that she could threaten you this way?"

"She was my queen."

Janet looked stunned. "Orlaith's sister was the *mad* queen?"

Eppa nodded. "And Queen Oonagh's cruelty was boundless. She possesses a book of dark magic that she regularly uses against her subjects.

No one is safe."

Janet's her hands flew to her mouth. She asked through her fingers, "Billy's ears?"

"Yes, and worse. Orlaith met another man, a human like your mother. She fell in love. Though my heart ached to see her love another, I saw her happy and that also brought my heart ease. John was kind and good and worthy of that love. I helped keep their relationship a secret, as did Billy. When Orlaith grew heavy with child and could no longer hide it from her sister, the queen became enraged. It was then Orlaith left the Aos Sidhe, intending to run away with John and live in his world. But Oonagh discovered them together that night and she murdered John. The horror caused Orlaith to give birth beside his body."

Janet shook her head, tears springing to her eyes.

"To add to the cruelty, Oonagh took the babe away as a changeling and brought another to the Aos Sidhe to live in his place. I did not know any of this until after the deed was done. Had I known I might have been able to help. Orlaith never told me her plan because she feared her sister's vengeance upon any who assisted her. I would have laid down my life for her escape." Haunted still by Orlaith's anguish, the emotion became too much. He squeezed his eyes shut and took a centering breath.

"How horrible for her, and for you."

Eppa nodded. "Orlaith remains in her sister's shadow of madness. I discovered where her babe was, safe with his father's family where Billy placed him. That was why I left the Aos Sidhe, to keep Oonagh from discovering the child's whereabouts through me."

"Billy was an accomplice in that treachery?"

He frowned. "Do not condemn him, Janet. More than once did Billy stand between certain death and Orlaith. Better he take the child away than have it murdered beside his father, no?"

She nodded.

"As it was, Oonagh discovered the child's location and sent him to steal the child back. Billy failed. Hobs are adept and competent creatures and I know our hob friend well. His failure to bring the boy to Oonagh was by design. To punish him, Oonagh cut off his ear with her dark magic. The queen has no idea the many of her evil plans that have failed because of him. She'd do far worse to him if she knew."

"Poor Billy. This is all so tragic. I feel so sad for you and Orlaith. And that poor changeling's family — "

Eppa raised his hands and cupped her face, and said sincerely, "Understand, I do *not* regret coming here and loving your mother for however brief that precious flame burned, for she gave me *you*. You have been the light in my life, and have been so since the moment I held you newly born."

Janet fell into his arms and sobbed softly against his chest.

He rocked her gently until her emotion was spent and her composure returned. When she straightened, he tipped her chin and met her eye once more. "I tell you this not to fill you with sadness or rouse my own. I tell you because *our* kind loves without hesitation. When our hearts engage, the love is true. There is no doubt when another captures our heart, no matter how brief the moment. We *know*."

Janet's cheeks pinked and Eppa suddenly knew the truth. It was as he suspected. His daughter *did* have feelings for Lenox.

She stammered, "I — I don't know *what* my feelings are."

Sensing she needed more time to come to terms with the truth of her emotions, he said, "I'm not referring to your feelings. I will only say this: If Lenox has offered you marriage, it is because his heart wants it. Not because he feels an obligation to do so. He's in love with you, my darling." He could feel her mind devouring his words.

Eyes growing large, she asked him, "Are you saying Lenox is like *us*?" Her eyes narrowed just as quickly. "Who is he, Papa?" Janet drew a sharp breath. Seized with apparent insight she didn't wait for his answer. She blurted, "He's the changeling!"

Eppa nodded. "Yes, Lenox is Orlaith's son, prince and heir to the throne of Aos Sidhe. And miraculously, the Lord of All has set his feet upon our doorstep."

~*~

At the end of Grant's Road, I caught sight of the lamplighter's bobbing light long before I saw him at work. Lighting all the lamps before the shop windows, he walked off on his stilts. All that remained was a vague flicker on the stabler's wall. I was reminded of a passage from Robert Louis Stevenson and could almost hear my mother's voice as she read it to me as a child:

> *My tea is nearly ready and the sun has left the sky;*
> *It's time to take the window to see Leerie going by;*
> *. . . For we are very lucky, with a lamp before the door;*
> *And Leerie stops to light it as he lights so many more.*

My momentary distraction did not last, however, as my mind returning to the fateful encounter at the stream. In all conscience, I couldn't see any other way this drama could have unfolded. I had stood alone against three men. Had I gone for fists, as had been my first impulse, I might have been rendered useless. What then? How else might I have come to her aid? Having thought long and hard on this, I knew there was no other option than what had occurred.

But none of it mattered now. My aid, well-motived as it was, unintentionally put the lady under a pall of shame and speculation. And tonight, when she realized this fact, how she felt was clear upon her face. She despised me for putting her in an indefensible situation. I saw the welcoming peg leg shingle in the glow of the gaslight. Chest hollow, I tied the horse to MacPhee's post and took myself inside, hoping a draft might pull me from the mire. What I got instead was a conversation in progress. Once I realized the topic, a fit of anger seized me.

Archie MacGilliveray scowled into his horn cup. "Ye should ha' seen her — shameless and naked as th' day th' good lord saw her born. An' she turned and looked me in th' eye and as good as said, take me Arch, make me yers. With her *husband* standin' near! Isn't tha' right, Georgie? Isn't it all th' way it was, her bein' bold as brass?"

The slight man looked uncomfortable with the lie, still he added to it clear enough when he said, "Yeah, Arch. Bold as brass, tha' one."

Archie drained his cup and slammed it down with such force the wooden bottom broke off with the impact and rolled across the bar. He raged, "Ye know, 'afore now I was never one t' believe th' auld tales. Ye know, 'bout her bein' a witch an' all. But I saw it in her tha' day. Turned me' blood t' ice, tha'. Janet Roxburgh o' whatere' she goes by now. Shameful tryin' t' make her *husband* a cuckold. The faithless wee bitch —"

Cutting off the ugly rant, Malcolm MacPhee growled, "*Damn ye!* I'll not hear another ill word about the lassie! And tha's the *second* cup ye broke! Ye'll no be breakin' more! Get out ye sorry liar!"

Archie growled, "I'm not *lyin'*! Th' whore witch promised t' me!"

MacPhee pulled a hatchet from behind the bar and slammed it down. "I told ye t' keep yer lyin' poison t' yerself! Go on yer way, damn ye. If I ha' t' say it again, ye'll be banned from this place fer th' whole length o' yer sorry life. *By god*, I swear it!" To the smaller man he railed, "Georgie Eams, damn ye t' hell, find yer balls ye friggin' eunuch. Take yer lyin' guid fer nothin' friend home."

Georgie pulled his friend's arm. "Come wi' me, Arch."

Archie turned on his stool and blinked when he saw me. Apparently ignorant of my identity, he pulled his arm from his fellow. Coming toward me menacingly, he said, "Ye're the bastard tha' stole *my* Janet!"

I heard the collective gasp.

Then MacPhee boomed, "Stand down ye bloody *hoormister!* Ye'll not address his lairdship that way!"

It all happened so fast from the moment I set foot inside. Furious, I flew at Archie. Taking him up by his collar, I shook him. "You'll start singing the truth of that day, you bleeding bastard, or I swear I'll do everything within a laird's power to see you transported." When he didn't talk, I shoved his head to the bar. With all my weight on his neck, I growled low at his ear. "Tell them, *damn you.* Tell them you're a filthy liar to talk about *my wife* this way!"

80

The collective surprise was palpable when the throng gasped. In that moment, nothing else mattered to me. He'd not shame her like this, not while I drew breath. He'd *admit* his treachery or by god I'd *beat* it out of him. Acknowledging that emotion, I felt an unmistakable vibration run through me.

Archie suddenly pleaded, "Stop! Whate'er yer doin', stop. I'll tell, I'll tell them it's all lies!"

I let him go. Lifting his head from the bar, he looked at me with fear shining bright in his eyes. To the throng gathered there, he said, "I didna know, I *didna* know Janet was Lady of Carterhaugh! I lied! It's lies, all o' them. Oh dear god, fergive me. I loved her." He covered his face in his hands and drunkenly sobbed. "I loved her me whole life. I'm so sorry, yer lairdship. I hope ye can forgive me. I'm so sorry Mac an' t' ye all. I loved her . . . jist loved, jist . . . . "

"Come on Archie, let's take ye away home," Georgie said and put an arm around the man's shoulders, and then led him out the door.

"I don' want t' see yer faces fer a month at least!" MacPhee called after the pair. Turning to me, he broke into a wide smile. He racked no less than a dozen small glasses on the bar, then proceeded to top them with whiskey. Rapid words laced with embarrassment poured forth, "Yer' lairdship! My Rosie said ye were down from Carterhaugh this afternoon. What'll ye ha' sir? I got me ales, an' a new cider now, since ye were last here. We've a fine single malt — *an dram buidheach* that is, an' it is a guid one. Stout gin an' aged whiskey too." First passing a glass to me and the rest around the room, he took the last for himself.

Raising his glass high, he said, "But first…To Laird Carter an' his new bride. She's a wonder an' a blessin' sir. May the best ye've ever seen, be the worst ye'll e'er see. May the mouse ne'er leave yer pantry wi' a teardrop in its eye! May yer hum keep blithely reekin', till ye're auld enough to die. May ye aye be jist as happy, as I wish ye both to be! *Slàinte mhòr agus a h-uile beannachd duibh!*"

The throng echoed, "*Slàinte mhath!*"

My ear for Scots still undeveloped, I had no idea what all was said. I felt the genuine wish for my good fortune with my new bride, however. I smiled and thanked them as two more rounds of toasts and whiskey made the room. The vibration of rage that ran through me, undoubtedly the cause of Archie's fear, dissipated with the second round. It was then I realized I'd neatly dug a hole for myself *again*, though I couldn't see how I might have wrung such an admission out of Archie without casting Janet upon the stage of derision.

I looked around the room and their genuine expressions of good cheer. These happy fellows might as well have been toasting my funeral.

TEN

I woke to a soft scraping sound that I rightly reasoned to be Winnet stirring the coals. The girl was generally as quiet as a church mouse and most days I slept through her visit. But today the scraping of metal on stone reverberated in an echo inside my throbbing skull. I heard myself groan.

"Oh! Guid mornin' t' ye, yer lairdship," came the happy greeting from the vicinity of the hearth.

I mumbled something and suddenly came aware that my mouth tasted like I'd curried a horse with my tongue. Winnet was chatting away at the window now. Trying to process the rapid Scots, I followed her with slitted eyes — a mistake that, for she drew the curtains back and the sunlight came at my brain like daggers. Rolling over, I burrowed into the linen and pored over fragments of memory, seeking an explanation as to why I felt like this. I had a vague recollection of being put to bed by Potts and before that, several good fellows seated me on my horse. Just why I needed such assistance came rushing back in blazing clarity.

My visit to MacPhee's Peg ended after I'd tipped round upon round of toasts to my good fortune as a married man. To some, I'd married a skilled healer held in high regard. To others, I'd married a witch who practiced the "auld ways." To Janet . . . I pressed my knuckles into my eye sockets. *Good lord, what had I done?* Hoping to stem the tide of words coming at me, I said, "Did you require something of me, Winnet?"

"Oh no sir, I was simply goin' t' ask, if I should ready her ladyship's chambers." She pointed to the large wall tapestry to her left. "They're right through there, yer lairdship. Th' door is hidden behind th' tapestry."

I groaned inwardly. It was exactly as I'd feared. The Laird of Carterhaugh marrying one of their own was newsworthy, and *all* of Selkirk must know my folly by now. I followed the girl's pointing finger to a depiction of hounds circling a mortally wounded boar. The skilled needlework led my mind to the inevitable outcome.

She added, "We ha' never had a Lady of Carterhaugh in all my years here, sir. But we can set her rooms t' rights in a jiffy. Should I tell Mrs. Frew ye wish t' make it so?"

With no way to bail my sinking ship without causing more turmoil, I said, "Yes, you do that."

She bobbed a curtsey and left me. A moment later, Potts entered with my shirt for the day and a fizzing glass of sodium bicarbonate. Handing it over, he said, "Good morning, sir. This will set you to rights. I've added a half-jigger of scotch for your head."

Nodding my thanks, I downed it quickly. Stifling the belch that came after, I ventured, "So, tell me the scuttle below stairs."

He smiled. "Well, from what I hear congratulations are in order. The house is buzzing like a beehive over your marriage, sir."

I sighed and dragged a hand over my face.

"Sir?"

"Yes?"

"Is it true then? Are you married to the midwife?"

I told him, "As far as everyone else here is concerned, yes I am. By the end of the day, I shall have a wife. One that hates me, I fear. Set my bath, and when you've finished here, send word to Samuel Ennis to saddle a horse. I'll leave within the hour."

"Yes, sir."

I eyed the tapestry so effectively hiding Lady Carter's chamber door. How I envied that boar.

~*~

Billy Blin called forth his glamour and transformed himself into an old crone.

Janet smiled at her father's longtime friend. Though it weren't obvious from his boyish personality, the hob was extremely old — older than her father's one-hundred-and-five years — and far older than the old woman Billy now portrayed. Papa said Billy's kind aged slowly, even slower than their kind. Her mind wandered with the thought.

She didn't know much about her kind. When she was a child, her father had occasionally shared bits and pieces of his life in the Aos Sidhe and Billy Blin often was a part of those stories. When Billy surprised them by showing up on their doorstep, she felt as though she already knew him. In the past several weeks she'd grown especially fond of the magical hob, in part because he was a wonderful gentle soul, but in greater part because her father missed his home and Billy was part of the life he once had. Her father loved Billy and she did too.

She asked, "Billy, do you take other forms beside the boy and this?"

He gave her a wizened grin through his disguise. "I've never had need, but were I to think on it a while I might have others." Sweeping his hands down his withered bosom, he asked with raised brows, "Would you rather not have Aunt Bedelia as your companion today?"

Janet kissed his cheek and handed him the smaller market basket. "I'd *love* your company no matter what form you take. Come along then, *Aunt Bedelia*, I've turnips and cheese to buy."

A short while later the pair wound their way through the market stalls. Janet picked over the bushels of turnips and selected a dozen of similar size before examining the beetroots. Billy sorted through several small round cabbages and placed two in his basket.

The cabbage farmer touched the brim of his hat and said to Billy, "Guid day, Mother Bedelia. Aye there's a lot o' fine cabbages today, m' missus says they're the best fer flavor this year."

"Yes, yes, yes, yer good wife is keen on 'er cabbages, Mr. Rankin. They *do* look foin. We'll take another." Billy giggled and dropped a smaller cabbage in the basket with the rest.

Spotting Janet, the farmer broke into a wide smile and swept the hat from his bald head. "An guid day t' ye, Lady Carter."

Dumbstruck by his words, Janet's heart began to pound as the man went on.

"I thought I might see ye fer market day, an so, I held these back." He uncovered a small basket of elongated eggs sitting on a handful of straw. "They're candled, they are. Double yolks all."

There was nothing to do but smile and see to the eggs Mr. Rankin brought especially for "Lady Carter" today. Inside, she steamed. *Blast you, Archie McGillivray.* Her heart leapt at hope: *Perhaps Archie had only spoken to Mr. Rankin alone?* But no sooner did she dare hope, when Mrs. Brown hurried over. "Oh yer ladyship, how guid it is t' see ye this sunny morn. I ha' a box o' pears fer ye, sweet as honey they are. My Rupert picked th' lot jist this morn."

Other well-wishers crowded around with goods brought to market in celebration, just for her. Janet met them all with a frozen smile, belying a mind in turmoil. Suddenly Billy was at her side, his hand on her basket handle, surreptitiously tugging her away from the throng. Far enough away as not to be heard, Janet asked him what was the matter.

"The young prince is coming."

Confused she asked, "A *prince*? Prince who?"

He jerked his head toward the end of the street, sending his bonnet askew.

Janet turned. Lenox Pendry, the changeling fae prince who didn't know who, or what he was, was riding their way.

Billy tugged harder, his words tumbled out in a panic. "We must away Janet, yes yes yes, we must!"

Janet frowned. Lenox had created this impossible situation. He'd meant well, she was sure of it. But now what? It would seem half the town thought them man and wife. She whispered, "I must play the game Archie set in motion, Billy, lest I be ruined. I *have* to talk to Lenox."

Billy thrust his basket of cabbage into her hands and ducked behind a stall. An instant later, the boy appeared. Taking it back, he said simply. "The young prince knows that face. I must use this one."

Prince. Her father's words came back to her. Lenox was just like her — half fae, half human. He had no idea he was a changeling. Was that even possible? Returning to the stalls, Janet continued her marketing, now with Billy the orphan in tow.

"Oh heavens, yer ladyship. Was yer auntie feeling poorly?" Mrs. Brown asked. "She left ye so sudden — "

Ignoring the title, Janet smiled. "Yes, Aunt Bedelia is under the weather this morning. She sent Billy to help me finish the marketing."

Mrs. Brown ruffled Billy's hair and gave him a small speckled pear. "An' this is fer yer trouble, Billy."

Eyes twinkling, Billy took a bite and said with a full mouth, "Thank y —"

Janet nudged him and admonished him. "Billy, you must chew and swallow before speaking." To Mrs. Brown she leaned close and whispered, "Do forgive his lapse in manners, Mrs. Brown. He's an orphan, you see."

"Aye, an so guid of Master Eppa t' take th' poor waif in. Yer papa worked wonders with my Charlie's lessons, he'll raise this pup right." Mrs. Brown pulled Billy into her ample bosom and gave him a hug. She said, "He's a guid laddie, there's no doubt in my mind ye are, Billy." Suddenly the woman's face broke into a wide smile as she looked past Janet's shoulder. "Oh yer lairdship! Guid morning t' ye sir."

Lenox tipped his hat. "Good morning, ladies, and to you, Billy."

Billy beamed and ate the core of his pear, seeds and all.

Mrs. Brown said happily, "I was jist talkin' wi' yer lady, sir. I brought a peck o' th' sweetest pears, an' gave Lady Carter th' first choice. My Rupert picked th' lot first light."

"They look fine indeed, Mrs. Brown," he said. "Your Rupert has a good eye for perfection." Lenox's smiling eyes went from Mrs. Brown to Mr. Brown, who stood behind his wife, smiling but saying nothing, to Janet, who raised her brows ever so slightly, inviting Lenox to play along. To her relief, he did.

He leaned from his horse and whispered conspiratorially, "Few know this, Mrs. Brown. But this lovely woman swept me off my feet and I begged her to become my wife. We married straight away in London this past August with little fanfare. And now I fear I must make amends to my new father-in-law, though my wife assures me he'll be pleased. Now that our secret is out, I'm sure my wife has much to tell him before she leaves for Carterhaugh. Don't you my love?"

Awash with relief, Janet smiled sweetly and nodded.

Jumping down from his horse, Lenox reached into his coat and withdrew his coin purse. Handing it to Billy, he said, "Finish the marketing will you, Billy?"

Billy hefted the jingling leather purse, and said happily, "I'll do that, Master Lenox." He skipped off with both nearly full baskets swinging.

Behind her, Janet heard Mr. Brown chuckle and say, "Tha' young pup sure ha' some muscle on 'im, though ye'd never know t' look at 'im."

To that his wife commented, "Aye, he' a strong laddie, wee as he is."

Lenox assisted Janet into the saddle. Taking the reins, he led the horse through the marketplace as well-wishers congratulated them on their marriage.

~*~

Given how she stormed off the night before, I half-expected Janet to rip the reins from my hand and trample me in her haste to be shot of me. Once we'd left the crowd behind, I dropped the reins. Without turning, I clucked my tongue and walked on. The horse followed.

Over my shoulder, I confessed, "I find I am at a loss for words."

She didn't respond and I felt an uncomfortable flutter in my belly. Pressing past the awkward moment, I explained my encounter at MacPhee's the night before. Again, she didn't say a word. Stopping, I turned to face her. The look of mortification on her lovely face amplified my guilt.

The sky had gone bluer with the sun's climb and now the morning light ran a thin ribbon of rainbow on the edges of the aura surrounding her. Only on rare occasion did I see auras of higher magnitude on people. In the last twenty-four hours, I'd seen three and they were all in the schoolmaster's house. Of these three, Janet's held the only rainbow.

Looking up, I met her violet eyes and told her sincerely, "I am *truly* sorry, Janet. Please believe me. I saw no other way to make him confess his lies without further bringing you harm. To my mind, his lies were damning your character."

Inscrutable now, she said, "I need to speak with my father."

"Of course." I clucked my tongue at the horse. Again he followed without my taking the reins.

"Do you have a way with all animals? Or with horses alone?"

I considered her question. Dudley and the Pendry horses always responded to me. Come to think, so did the sheep that Brookes tended for the lawns. Even the ram that routinely charged and butted everyone else would frolic like a lamb for a pat from my hand. And then there was Argus. The peacock came from Mother's Indian tea connection. The bird had often sat in the tree outside my bedroom window when I was a boy. Ever protective, Mother discovered I'd been climbing out on the limb to sit with him and so she had him sent to the Wallingford's before I could "fall and break my neck." When the bird somehow traveled twenty-six miles, back to my bedroom window, Mother allowed me to keep him, provided I *not* sit in the treetop again. Smiling with memories of home, I answered Janet by sharing that story. To my delight, she laughed. I fought the urge to turn to her again.

She said, "Argus? Named for the giant with one hundred eyes from Greek mythology?"

"One and the same. A fine name for boy to name a peacock, don't you think? I'd read about Argus in *Bulfinch's Mythology*."

"I love Bulfinch's. Papa teaches his students from it."

Grateful for her light conversation, I smiled and explained, "Our butler's personal library is quite impressive. The man's keen on mythology — Greek,

Roman, Norse, any and all mythology, really. He finds the fairie world of these British Isles especially intriguing."

"It's rather curious he'd have such a study, don't you think?"

I'd never given Osgood's interest thought beyond my personal fascination with it. "I don't think it odd, the mind will have its pursuits no matter one's occupation," I said. "Our cook is an accomplished concertina player, and one of our Pendry footmen is an artist of no little talent."

The schoolhouse lay ahead. I had no idea how this day would unfold but our course of action had been clear enough in the marketplace. Janet was as deep in the charade today as I had been at MacPhee's Peg last night. Perhaps we could pretend to live as man and wife at Carterhaugh and when I returned to Pendry .... My heart seized at the thought of never seeing her again and I instantly cast the idea aside. I knew what my ideal was: I was incomprehensibly in love with this woman I barely knew. Despite that fact, I wouldn't press myself upon her again, as she'd made her opinion plain enough last night. But willingly or otherwise, we were thrown together by fate. Hopefully her father could sort this out.

~*~

Turning to the crash, Eppa found Billy in his natural state — lying belly-down on a small mound of cabbages and turnips with a straw-packed box of eggs, cradled in his hands unharmed. He rushed to help Billy to his feet. Knowing it wasn't in the nature of hobs to be clumsy, he asked, "What is it, Billy?"

Long spindly fingers grasping, Billy put the spilled vegetables back in the basket in a flash. He said breathlessly, "The young prince comes!"

"Now?"

"Yes yes yes! He comes with Janet. I've wonderful news, my dear friend, the village believes them married!"

Eppa dragged a hand over his face. Hearing the nicker of the horses in the paddock, he turned to Billy. "They'll be at the door soon, Billy. You'd best hie yourself to the kitchen."

"I'll put the kettle on. The young prince might enjoy a cup of mugwort tea," Billy said, and with that took himself to the kitchen where he hummed happily as he worked.

Eppa stared absently at the closed kitchen door, his thoughts awhirl. Billy's hopeful exuberance aside, his daughter's heart may have softened with the truth of Orlaith's son, but that didn't mean she'd agree to be Lenox's wife.

The front door opened and Janet rushed in. She went straight into his arms. "Papa!"

Eppa hugged his daughter and ran a soothing hand on her back. Over the top of her head, he met Lenox, who offered a slight nod and a weary smile. The young man looked wretched. Waving him in, Eppa told him, "Please, come inside."

Sniffling, Janet said, "Excuse me, I'll return shortly." With that she hurried up the stairs to her room.

Eppa turned to see Billy entering with a full tea tray in his spindly-fingered hob hands. Apparently catching himself at the last second, the glamour sparkled over him an instant before his boy's full disguise materialized. Eppa said, "Billy has brought us tea, Lenox. Will you share a cup?"

Turning to the boy in surprise, Lenox remarked, "Yes, thank you. What a quick fellow you are, Billy. We only just left you at the market."

Eppa said, "Yes, our Billy is an efficient lad."

Billy laughed with delight and filled their cups.

Lenox explained in detail the encounter at MacPhee's the night before and at the market that morning. He added, "I meant to protect your daughter, sir. But I fear I have complicated all our lives in the process."

Eppa considered the intent behind the action, and again it spoke volumes about the man Orlaith's son had grown to be. In fact, his gallantry was reminiscent his grandfather, King Ruaraidh. Giving an encouraging smile, Eppa told him, "I would have done the same, son."

Lenox exhaled slowly, his relief obvious.

"And now we are left to determine what we'll do next. Another place, another time, our course of action would be clear," he said, his words trailing off with his thoughts. Eppa often longed to return to the Aos Sidhe and he wished he were there now. There his daughter would not be condemned for societal rules devised centuries ago by wrong-minded men who sought to usurp the auld ways. There she wouldn't be held to spurious conventions that would declare her a fallen woman simply because she lived naturally, as any fae would. Thinking of the world his daughter should have been born to, he frowned. With Oonagh in power, only the Goddess knew the state of the Aos Sidhe today. He'd never bring his daughter near that madness. With few options, he'd adhered to the customs of this human world and that meant protecting his daughter's standing in the community.

"Master Eppa?"

"Hmm? Oh, forgive me. My mind was searching the clouds for answers."

"If I may speak plainly, sir," Lenox said, "I do see one solution."

"Yes?"

"It concerns my remaining time at Carterhaugh. I plan to return home to Pendry at the end of October — "

The sound of china shattering on the hearth's flagstones interrupted the conversation. Both men turned toward Billy, who had already went down on hands and knees, gathering the shards of his broken cup. He stood, nodded an apology, then hurried into the kitchen where his distress could be heard clearly.

Concern written upon his face, Lenox said, "Has the boy injured himself, do you suppose?"

Eppa shook his head. Billy knew as well as Eppa did that Lenox was in danger if he returned to Pendry before the first day of November. "Billy doesn't wish you to leave," Eppa said. "I believe the lad has grown attached to you, Lenox. He'll be fine after his emotions vent themselves. Now, you were saying that you plan to leave?"

Nodding, Lenox said, "Yes, I only planned to be here as long as it took to settle my uncle's estate. Recently I thought I might stay."

"For Janet?"

Lenox looked him in the eye. "Sir, may I speak plainly?"

"Of course."

Setting his cup aside, Lenox said, "In truth, I'd be the happiest man alive were your daughter to return my affection. I've been head over heels since the moment we met. I've had my answer, however. Janet will not consent to become my wife, and I will abide. But were she to live at Carterhaugh under the guise of Lady Pendry, the talk in the village would cease." He quickly added a vow, "I assure you, she would have every privacy. She need not suffer my presence overmuch, and with care, the servants need never know of the charade. And when I leave, she'll have the manor and lands as her own, to do with as she sees fit. I'll not return to muddy the waters. My time here will fade from memory."

Eppa considered the young prince's words and noted the edge of sadness. The night before he'd had an insight to his daughter's feelings for this man. They were two of a kind, half human and half fae. Given time, their fae blood would lead them quickly from attraction to love. As far as he could tell, this had already occurred, they were indeed already in love.

The sobbing in the kitchen grew louder then abruptly stopped. Eppa tilted his head slightly and listened, his fae hearing detecting no sound at all. Like all hobs, Billy had an affinity for livestock and had a special bond with Janet's goat. He might have sought comfort in the stable. Eppa returned his attention to the young man beside him.

~*~

In a swirl of glitter, Billy Blin materialized beside a startled Janet. She squeaked in surprise.

"Oh Janet, this is terrible, just *terrible*!" He said, sitting down on a corner of her bed and sobbing quietly into his spindly hands.

Sitting down beside him, she offered a comforting pat on his back. "What has happened?"

"The young prince! He plans to return to Pendry. No, no, *no, he mustn't* do that!"

"Why?" she asked, brows knitting together. "Why can't Lenox return home?"

The little creature's large eyes grew larger and he shook his head, as though he'd already said too much.

Janet, as perceptive as any fae, felt awash in understanding. Billy wasn't aware she knew the truth. She said, "It's alright. Papa told me that Lenox is a changeling and doesn't know what or who he is."

Appearing relieved by her words, Billy held out a hand and an enormous lace-edged handkerchief sparkled into being. He blew his nose with a loud wet honk. Meeting her eyes, he said, "Oh it's far worse, Janet dear, far far *far* worse."

"Whatever do you mean?"

Billy explained Queen Oonagh's deadly obsession with her nephew and the Ride to Tithe at the end of the year. He explained the archaic plan to murder Lenox the day before his birthday in exchange for wishes.

Stunned, Janet blinked. "You're saying he'll be *killed* if he returns?"

Billy nodded and dabbed fresh tears with his handkerchief. Suddenly, he jumped up and blurted, "But he'd stay for you!"

She stared at him.

Billy pressed, "Do you not *see* the love the young prince has for you? That love would keep him here, keep him safe. Yes yes yes, it would!"

Lenox had gone out of his way to help her with Archie, although this made a larger problem for both of them. In truth, she'd been thinking about Lenox since first she set eyes on him at the Roxburgh ruins. Fondness had grown since he came to her aid at the river, and especially so on their walk from the market. He had proposed marriage. Was it really love and not action spurred by a sense of duty? It couldn't it be. She scoffed lightly, "Billy, we've only recently met . . . ."

He reached for her hand. Giving her fingers a gentle squeeze, he explained what he knew of fae. "When love is near, your kind falls quickly. The heart knows this long before the mind confirms it. A fae knows with certainty when their heart has found love. And my kind can see the love light."

"Love light? You mean an aura?" Papa had told her that hobs possessed different abilities than fae. It made sense. They were different creatures after all. She knew all living things had a light and whether or not it was vibrant depended upon health. In all the years of her healing, she'd never seen a variation that did not belong to the sick or the dying. Outside of her father and Billy, who both had naturally strong auras, the light was the same for all life, except for Lenox. His aura was more a rainbow of color.

Billy nodded. "Yes, the aura. For lovers, the love light is a rainbow that shines the same on both."

Rainbow? She swallowed. She'd seen that multicolored aura on Lenox when he came to her aid, and today it was even brighter. This meant Lenox was truly in love? A sudden thought came to her. She asked, "Did Orlaith and Papa share a love light when you last saw them together?"

Billy smiled with a quivering lip. A single tear ran down his cheek. "They did."

Papa loved Orlaith and she loved him in return. Janet drew a deep breath and let it out slowly. Making up her mind, she decided she'd do everything in her power to keep Lenox here. To the hob, she said, "I'll go to Carterhaugh and I'll manage to convince Lenox to stay until his birthday passes. But Billy, I can't promise more."

He rocked on his heels happily and said with a grin, "No need, no need. You have feelings for the young prince, dear Janet. I see that you do. Those feelings are new, yes, but they are the same for him. See?" He held his palm out several inches from her body and pulled his hand back slowly. A sparkling light grew between them and she saw the rainbow edge of her aura where it touched his.

Realization brought about an odd fluttering sensation in her belly. Janet felt her cheeks grow warm. She went to her wardrobe and found the largest valise. Turning to Billy, she said, "I need to pack. I'll be down shortly."

The room filled with glitter and suddenly every item of clothing, every toiletry she owned, and all her medicinals were packed by magic. She tested how heavy her valise was and found it weighed virtually nothing. She laughed lightly and thanked him.

He smiled and shifted into the boy again.

~*~

Feeling Janet's presence at the doorway, Eppa and I turned at once to see her standing with valise in hand. This she set on the floor and came to join us. Billy, apparently in a much better frame of mind, rushed in with a cup of tea and thrust it into her hands. His smile brought to mind the cat that ate the canary.

Her father went to embrace her. I couldn't make out the words he said at her ear, but I heard her say, "Yes, Papa. I know." In that moment, I watched their auras expand and brighten. I'd never seen the like before. Even little Billy, who stood near, brightened. Though all three were my recent acquaintances, I was met with a rush of affection and warmth for headmaster and the boy that I could not begin to describe, as curiously quick upon me as the love I felt for the fair witch who was about to pretend to be my wife

ELEVEN

O rlaith sat under the shade of the sprawling sacred ash tree and took Amelia's locket from its place near her heart. Opening it, she gazed upon the small photographs of Lenox the child and Lenox the man he'd become. Her all-consuming aloneness lightened a bit. The was no doubt in her mind that the human world had magic of its own, for here in the face of their son she saw the likeness of his father. It was almost as if she had their essence here, side by side. She ran a fingertip wistfully over the image of Lenox as a boy and felt a mother's pride. He smiled with his eyes exactly as John did so often. Snapping the locket closed, she tucked it inside her gown. *John.* Their love had been brief but true.

So many loved ones were forever gone from her life and her world was so very small without them. It was clear Oonagh was falling deeper into her madness. Time and again, Oonagh inflicted her cruelty on those Orlaith cared most for. Now, through this lonely, self-imposed isolation, she kept them all safe.

Her thoughts returned to Billy. For the length of her life the dear hob had been a presence. Bound by the unconditional love and devotion that was the nature of his kind, he had looked after her mother's family further back than even she knew.

She was confident Billy would seek Eppa's whereabouts. She wondered if he'd actually found him, and if so, how Eppa was. From her earliest days, she'd loved Eppa for the friend he was, but it wasn't until he left did she realize the depth of her feelings. She missed him terribly.

A rowanberry dropped on her head. She looked up to find a small snow bunting tugging at a bunch of ripening berries. The next berry hit her square in the forehead. She laughed and held out a finger. The little bird flew there and dropped a small curl of paper into her lap before flying up to perch on her shoulder.

"What is this, little friend?"

Orlaith unrolled the scroll and the paper grew in size. She smiled at the recognizable flourish of the pen. It was a letter from Billy. She read:

> *Old friends have found one another and it is safe and warm.*
> *You have no reason to stay and every reason to come. Will you?*

The little bird hopped up and down on her shoulder. Billy often shared secrets with birds. In fact, he'd taught her this skill when she was a child. Orlaith tipped her head to give the bird her ear in case there was more the letter couldn't say. The plump little bird chittered away. Her eyes grew large. Thanking the bunting with a kiss on his small feathered head, she watched him fly away.

She hurried to the hill and walked through the glittering charm concealing the Aos Sidhe from the human world. At her chamber door, Orlaith met Flann the Urisk. She couldn't help but notice the odd tilt to his head, which was due to the fact his left horn had been sawed off. Now that Billy had fled, Oonagh took her wrath out on the poor faun. She greeted him.

His goat feet clicked on the stone flags and he bowed. "Greetings, my lady. The queen bids you come at once."

She touched the shorter horn and said, "I am so very sorry for this."

He covered her hand with his hoof and gave her fingers a light squeeze, conveying that he understood. She turned and walked away. The sound of his hooves clattered all the way to the kitchens.

~*~

Knowing her sister held court each morning, Orlaith found Oonagh where she'd thought she'd be, in the throne room. She bowed her head briefly, before asking, "You sent for me, sister?"

"I did." Oonagh smiled. "Why haven't I seen you at court?"

Orlaith regarded her. The smile didn't light those dark brown eyes and no warmth was reflected there. Long ago, she'd realized her sister's smile was nothing more than pretense; as superficial as the garments she wore. She replied, "There is no one I wish to see."

The smile disappeared. "I am queen and you are my sister."

Orlaith shook her head. "Yes, *you* are queen, Oonagh. And I am not needed at court."

"Appearances, Orlaith! I am not *requesting* your presence, I expect it. Your nonattendance reflects poorly upon the throne. *My* throne. "

Orlaith gave a small bow of her head. Family or not, enemies or not, the queen ruled and as long as she remained in the Aos Sidhe, she must obey her. Fortunately, she was leaving.

Oonagh's smile returned. "I expect your help in planning for the Samhain celebration."

Knowing Oonagh's plans for Lenox, Orlaith stiffened but quickly composed herself. Oonagh was unaware that Orlaith had any knowledge of Lenox. That her sister would expect her participation in planning a celebration that would include her own son's sacrifice indicated a deeper insanity than anyone knew. In a display of compliance, she tipped her head again. With a smile of her own, she said, "Of course, sister, though it is some distance in the future. Will that be all?"

Oonagh paused as if she had something else to say but changed her mind. She waved her hand dismissively. "For now."

With that, Orlaith returned to her rooms with plans to make.

~*~

Oonagh watched Orlaith go. Generally, bending her sister to her will amused her. But her sister's unanticipated acquiescence left her feeling off-balance. Her thoughts were redirected by her changeling.

"I am here, Mother. And this is for you." Rowan kissed her cheek before handing her a pale blue harebell. "You've summoned me?"

She smiled for his flower and motioned for him to sit upon the dais beside her throne. "Yes, dear boy. Have you observed your aunt of late?" She picked up the flower and examined the sprig. One of the bell flowers was more wrinkled than the others. Hiding her frown, she proceeded to gently rake her fingers through the boy's ginger hair as genuinely as a mother might.

"Yes, she travels above ground often. As far as I am able to determine, she spends her time simply sitting in the grove."

Fingers paused, Oonagh's brows drew together. "Doing what?"

Rowan shrugged. "Reading, tying knots, sketching, nothing of interest or note. I've watched her often since the day your hob disappeared."

She resumed petting his head, and asked, "You are certain, nothing out of the ordinary?"

He shook his head. "Nothing at all really, she keeps to herself . . . Although, I did see her with her head bent to a bird on her shoulder, as if she were listening to it."

The fingers curled into his scalp. He yelped, "*Ow!* Mother, you're hurting me. What is it?"

She pulled her hand away. At the snap of her fingers, a glass sphere materialized in her hand. She handed it to her changeling. She told him, "From this moment forward, you are to follow my sister. Do you understand? You are not to let her out of your sight. When you have news, you speak it to this orb and it will come to me."

Rowan tucked the orb into his pocket, and then rubbed his scalp. "Yes, Mother, of course. Why would you have me follow — ?"

Oonagh barked, "— Yours is not to question *me*, child. Now do as your queen tells you! Go!"

He frowned but nodded. "Yes, Mother."

Alone, Oonagh spit, "Talking with *a* bird? Oh Billy, do you think I'd not know the bird was sent by *you*? Orlaith will go to you and when she does, I will know it. When I find you, my traitorous hob, you will pay a dear price for your treachery."

Crushing the harebell in effigy, she tossed it aside.

~*~

Orlaith moved around her chambers with purpose, seeking only those items that held precious memories. All in all, there was little to take with her. She wrapped a small bundle and tucked it safely away for tomorrow night. The bunting said Billy was with Eppa, and unbelievably, so was Lenox. And she was going to them.

In all the long years of her life, only twice did she consider leaving the Aos Sidhe — the first after that horribly cruel night at her sister's hand, and again after Eppa left. Because she was born to the hereditary line, she stayed out of duty, for upon Oonagh's death the crown would fall to her. She warmed as a different thought took her. The bloodline belonged to her son and the Aos Sidhe would be his to cherish one day.

Travel in the human world required the coin they used. She penned a quick note to Amelia, knowing she would help her. Perhaps even lend her a horse. Most horses loved to leave their pastures for the change of scenery such jaunts provided. The humans would simply believe their horse had escaped the paddock and hope for its return. The borrowed horse would always return; no worse for wear and infinitely happier. On rare occasion when fae needed to travel, they'd call upon a horse to assist them, but she didn't dare call the nearby horses to her aid. She knew Oonagh was not above tormenting those poor creatures to discover her whereabouts.

She folded the note and pressed it to her heart. Focusing her thoughts, she sent it on in a golden shimmer of light.

~*~

Amelia Pendry sat before her desk working on the guest list for her upcoming art gala. Fanny entered the room with several freshly-laundered undergarments over her arm. As if her maid were privy to the conversation happening in her mind, Amelia said, "No, Mr. Brumbaton would make everyone at table six uncomfortable with his incessant political views. Wouldn't he, Fanny?"

Without missing a beat, the lady's maid said, "The man *is* a conversationalist, my lady."

Amelia made a disparaging snort. "Exactly. No one wants a second war with the Boers, nor do they want to hear of it while they dine. I simply don't know where to put the man. I wouldn't even invite him if not for his steady patronage of the arts."

Fanny said, "Didn't Master Lenox suggest Mr. Brumbaton be seated with other military men at the last gala, my lady?"

"Yes he did! I'll seat him at table eight with Colonel Parker and his wife. If anyone has opinions about the Boers, it is Colonel Parker. Him with that ghastly artificial leg he keeps his flask in. Excellent solution, Fanny. Thank you. "

At the door, Fanny said, "I'm always happy to help if I can, my lady." With that she closed the door behind her.

Satisfied that her son would approve, Amelia finished her list. Lenox had fair diplomacy when placing difficult guests at dining tables and she sorely missed his input as well as his company.

A small light at her window caught her attention as it brightened and pulsed. Fireflies and glow worms certainly didn't do that. Curious, she opened the window and watched as a small shimmering ball floated onto the desk and transformed itself into a note. Seeing it was from Orlaith, she sat and read.

Dearest Amelia,

A friend bids me to come to him, but I cannot travel in your world easily without my sister's notice. I seek to borrow coin as well as a mount. The horse will be returned to you shortly. I am most anxious to go. I will wait for you in your stable at midnight with greater news. Lenox is there!

Ever Your Friend,

Orlaith

Amelia frowned at her reflection. She understood Orlaith's desire to see Lenox. But as far as he knew, his only mother was sitting right here. Would Orlaith be content to simply meet him as a friendly stranger? If not, what would Lenox say if he knew the truth?

She told the mirror, "He'd be shocked of course."

Would such news matter if he knew he was still a Pendry? And that his Uncle John was his father and not Evan? After all, he'd never known either, only what she'd shared about them through the years. She read the note again and a tear marred the ink. She couldn't imagine Lenox disdaining her, the truth of his birth aside. She had raised him on her mother's love and knew he loved her in return. Still, a small knot of fear sat heavy on her heart, fear of hurting him.

She wiped her eyes then tossed the note upon the fire where it burned with an odd purple flame.

~*~

Having seen an orb of light pass through his aunt's door and fly down the hall, Rowan chased after it. It led him out of the Aos Sidhe and through field, woods, and pasture. A covey of quail flew in his face to startle him. What was it about birds lately? One spoke with his aunt and made mother furious to hear of it.

The orb gained speed when it neared the village. He ran as fast as he could, but it continued on, disappearing in the direction of the large estate just beyond. Winded, he hunched over, hands on knees, struggling to catch his breath before resuming the chase. A nightingale landed atop his head and dropped a leaf down the back of his shirt. He shooed it away before shaking the leaf from his clothing. He stood up straight, ready to continue down the village's tiny high street in the direction of the orb, when two women gasped as they caught sight of him.

Rowan heard the younger one say, "Mama, he's the spitting image of Papa, only ginger like Patrick!" Rowan turned to them. The older woman stared at him with wide eyes. She said, "May I ask, what is your name, young man?"

Before anyone could say more, a male voice came from inside the shop as a man apparently approached the doorway. "Libby, I forgot to tell you that Lady Pendry has ordered hot cross buns for her luncheon tomorrow, more than one hundred. I'll need you here. Bess can see to little Maisy and Martin . . . . " The baker trailed off when he realized his wife and daughter stood with their back to him, their attention elsewhere. He came out the door and came around, to see they were staring wide-eyed at a ginger-haired young man, a man whose face he saw in the mirror each morning when he shaved his whiskers.

Rowan smiled and walked on.

Bess kissed her father's cheek, whispering, "He looks just like you, only with Patrick's ginger hair." With that she turned on her heel, and as she hurried home she called out, "And I'll watch the twins, Papa!"

Waiting for their daughter to be out of earshot, Libby flew to her husband in disbelief. That red-haired young man had the same gapped front teeth as he!

Mr. Benton asked his wife, "*Who* was that?"

Libby shook her head, confusion thick in her voice as she said, "I-I don't know . . . do *you* know? He *looks* like he could be *your son*!"

Reading an inexplicable range of emotion — including condemnation — in her eyes, the baker frowned and said, "Here now! I've never laid eyes on tha' young man before. And all my sons I share with you and you alone, my heart. Even our boy in heaven only knew you as his mother."

Inexplicably, Libby fell into his arms and cried.

The baker patted his wife's back. "Libby, love, what's the matter?"

Overcome with emotion, she hiccupped, "I don't know, Danny. I don't know."

~*~

Rowan felt odd. *That human's face* . . . he probed the similar gap between his front teeth with the tip of his tongue. It was as if he'd seen his own reflection in the mirror, but older. And that woman! He'd had an overwhelming desire to wrap his arms around her. That he didn't left him with an ache in his heart.

With the Pendry mansion in sight, he sat under a tree while a wave of sadness enveloped him. For no reason he could discern, he sobbed.

A short time later, after pulling himself together, he crept along the stable wall. His aunt had come, and a few minutes after that, a human woman from the house joined her in the stable. He pressed his ear to the outer wall and frowned, realizing he could hear very little. The door suddenly opened and his aunt came out on a horse. The woman following said, "I shall join you in Selkirk in a fortnight. Please make certain Lenox is not hurt by, by all of this."

Orlaith said, "I would die before I brought him pain. Rest assured, dear Amelia."

Rowan waited until he was alone then took the glass orb from his pocket and whispered to it. He opened his hand the sphere took off in a flash of silver. For the first time, he wondered why he needed such a device. Others in the Aos Sidhe could send their own messages, but he was never able to do so. For all of his life he'd wondered when his magic would come. Mother always said he was coming late to his gifts, just as she had. Thinking of the queen, his thoughts surprisingly went to the baker and his wife. He found himself wanting to know them.

TWELVE

Not one pair of hands sat idle at Carterhaugh. In whirlwind haste, the entire household staff tidied the manse from top to bottom. The older girls picked from the herb garden and wove lavender for the bureau drawers. Even the youngest children were sent to pick wildflowers from the hillside.

Glynnis Frew saw to it that the lady's chambers were clean, comfortable, and aired adequately. Fortunately they adhered to the quarterly cleaning schedule set in place by the first lady at Carterhaugh. But two months past, the rooms had been thoroughly cleaned. Winded from the work, the housekeeper sat down to catch her breath. If Mrs. Nevin hadn't heard it from Mrs. Brown at the market that morning, she never would have known the new laird was bringing home his bride today. And what kind of greeting would a dusty, stuffy room have made for sweet Janet, their new Lady Carter? *Lady Pendry*, she reminded herself. There hadn't been a lady here since Laird Charles's own mother. After Laird Charles's sweetheart succumbed to consumption before they could wed, the poor man's broken heart never ventured for love again. Yes, a lady in the house would be a breath of fresh air. Especially this lady.

Glynnis took a measure of pride that it was likely her letter to Master Eppa that set the wheels in motion. Still, it came as a surprise to hear they'd fallen in love this quickly. Janet and the young laird had only just met, though the story was going around that they'd married secretly earlier in the summer. Well, they were cut from the same cloth, after all. Perhaps that was the way of fae and the half-blooded. Perhaps their kind knew love at first sight. Perhaps. However it came to be, she couldn't have dreamed better for them. Glynnis smiled. They were well-matched beyond their faerie blood. Outlander he may be, but Laird Lenox was a fine man destined to make a fine husband.

The breakfast table had buzzed with news. The night before, the young laird gave that scoundrel Archie MacGilliveray the dressing down the man so richly deserved. And good for it, too. The reprobate had chased the poor lassie's skirts for far too long.

Winnet smoothed the top coverlet on the bed. Turning to the housekeeper, she said, "I'm so happy fer her, Mrs. Frew, but it'll be hard t' remember Janet is now the Lady of Carterhaugh. Isn't tha' th' truth, Mary?"

Mary laughed lightly, "Och, I know. I've been imagining her with her hair all done up fancy an' wearin' silk, so I can ha' th' right thought in m' mind when I see her next. An' I'm hoping his lairdship doesna take insult if it takes more'n a few days t' ha' it drummed into my head."

"I don't think his lairdship is that way, Mary," Winnet said, shaking her head. "D' ye think it, Mrs. Frew?" Without pausing for the answer, she added, "Janet an' I always chatted when she came. I'll miss that. I suppose we'll learn our place with her soon enough."

The housekeeper said, "Just smile and do yer work, lassies. If ye keep yer mouths closed until ye don't ha' t' think about it, the new order of things will take root."

Young Boyd Nevin stood in the doorway and cleared his throat. "Pardon me, Mrs. Frew, me mam put th' bunch o' heather I picked in this vase. She said ye'd know where it is I should set it, but wha' e'er I do, she said I'm to stay off th' Aubusson."

Glynnis smiled. "There's a good laddie, t' know ye shouldna' walk on carpet with those hobnailed boots."

Mary hurried to take the bouquet and set it on the bedside table. She asked, "What will ye ha' me do next, Mrs. Frew?"

Before she could speak, the head butler peered into the room. "Mrs.

Frew, a word please."

She dismissed the maids and the lad, and then looked at the butler expectantly.

"Hamish Ennis sent word from his middle son," he explained. "Apparently Davy's been fishing all morn for eels for Ruthie."

"Yes, she told me she ha' asked his lairdship if there were any meals he'd like her t' try. He said he was never one for heavy meats. So to surprise him, she plans t' make an eel pie."

"Oh tha's good, good," he said with a nod.

"So, ye didna find me t' talk of eels." She raised her brows.

Munro chuckled. "No, tha's not why I came fer ye. Davy was taking th' short route o'er the hill, an' saw his lairdship and our new Lady Carter awa' in th' distance. By now, they'll ha' neared th' main road, an' will be arriving shortly. I've sent young Boyd to the dovecote t' watch th' drive. We'll greet her ladyship properly as is her due."

~*~

At the window on the second floor landing, young Boyd kept his eye on the gate at the far end of the drive. Spying the laird and his bride, he called down the stairway to his sister, "Betty, go tell Mr. Munro 'ere they come!"

The girl ran to relay the message.

Servants came rushing from all corners of the manse and lined up in the foyer with the sexes across from one another. Munro went down the line as shirts were tucked, aprons smoothed, and caps and collars adjusted. He said, "Aye, look sharp. Good, good."

Holding his elbow out to the housekeeper, he escorted Mrs. Frew outside. The other servants fanned out on either side of the door, gamesmen, groomsmen, and grounds men to his right, butlers, footmen, maids, cook, and kitchen staff on her left. The handful of children, scrubbed as bright as new pennies, all held a single flower for their new lady to build a welcome bouquet with.

Satisfied with the presentation, Munro told them, "Aye, that'll do. Now, dinna ye ferget, Miss Janet is Lady Pendry now. 'Tis best ye hold yer tongue until spoken to, fer as long as it take's ye t' remember tha' fact." He raised a bushy brow at Winnet and Mary. Pink cheeked, both young women grew suddenly interested in their shoes.

~*~

Janet barely uttered a word all the long ride to Carterhaugh, and not for lack of trying on my end to stir conversation. In the strained silence, the deep and terrible truth of my unrequited love became obvious to me. It was likely Janet resented me for what I'd unintentionally coerced her to do.

We passed the gates and rounded the bend. The house came into view. Trying once more to break the silence, I said, "It's my understanding you were born here."

"Yes, my birth was quite the sad scandal."

My shoulders slumped. My dealings with this woman were akin to walking barefoot through an unmucked stable. How was it I managed to foul every turn? To my surprise, she went on.

"As the heir, my mother's brother controlled their household. He took issue with my impending birth and sent her away. There was an ice storm that night and deep snow under that, but he made her leave regardless."

"Sounds a right callous chap."

"According to Papa, he was. Apparently his unpleasant temperament was made worse by fondness for whiskey. My mother walked all the way here, knowing Selkirk was too far and Laird Charles would see her safe. Her condition was such when she arrived half-frozen that there was little strength left for the rest."

Her response had a clinical tone, perhaps because of her calling, or perhaps because she'd never known her mother, as I had never known my father. Save for a wistful wish otherwise, there was no emotion to expend on the unknown. I shared the little I knew of my father.

"And what of your mother?" Janet asked.

"She is alive and well at Pendry."

"Do you resemble your father?"

"The Pendry men several generations back all share a strong family resemblance. Going by portraits and photographs, I see more of my Uncle John than my father when I look in the mirror. When I was a boy, I'd often hear mention of a striking similarity to him. I owe my eye coloring to my mother's side, I suppose. I'm told the Pendry men all had hazel eyes. Hers are green."

The conversation stopped there.

"Everyone knows?" she asked a few minutes later.

Confused, I asked her to clarify.

She pointed in the distance. "See? The staff is at the door. Do they know I'm pretending to be your wife?"

Sure enough, the entire staff was out to greet us, the newlyweds. "Pretending? No. Even my manservant believes we've married as of this morning. Potts is the soul of discretion; I trust his silence where others are concerned. At the market, when I shared with Mrs. Brown that we'd eloped, I knew Mrs. Nevin would soon hear of it. Today is her market day as well. That the household stands ready to greet you says they believe the story as I've told it, that the deed was done months ago."

"So that's why you said all that this morning."

"I was only trying to protect your good name. It was a spur of the moment strategy, I assure you."

She gave me a smile, a *genuine* smile, and said, "I know you only meant well, Lenox. I understand, and I thank you for your intent."

I considered her words. Taking a chance, I nudged my horse beside hers and reached for her hand. Janet took mine and a tingling rush raced up my arm and danced over my heart. I added, "I promise you, this will be painless. You'll not suffer my presence any more than necessary to assure you're well-situated when I leave here. I agree it is insufficient compensation for all you've suffered at my hand, but if we're careful to show affection toward one another in public, no one will guess our charade. It's especially important the household staff believe we are man and wife. Their knowledge will be shared in the market and pub. None will be the wiser."

I wasn't going to pass on a chance to show affection to the woman I loved, however insincere her return might be. For a short while I would live my dream and hope like hell my poor heart could take the strain.

~*~

Munro stepped forward to greet the young laird and his lady. In the flurry of efficiency that followed, the horses were led away to the barn and Janet's luggage hustled inside.

Lenox offered her his arm and then greeted the throng. "I've brought my new bride home. I'm certain you'll see to her care as you have seen to mine."

Collecting the last of her bouquet, Janet smiled and said, "I've known most of you for the whole length of my life. Though circumstances have indeed changed, I hope you would continue to seek me out to treat your ills, just as you have in the past." She took the housekeeper's hand affectionately. "You look very well today, Mrs. Frew."

The elder beamed. "Thank ye, yer ladyship. I've never felt better. It's *so* guid t' have ye here at Carterhaugh."

THIRTEEN

In my short absence, Mrs. Frew and Munro saw the manse gleaming. Spotless to begin with, the old place took on a vital quality. In my rooms the first thing I noticed was that the boar tapestry had been removed to facilitate a laird's easy access to his lady. If only our prevarication were true.

I could hear a melody of voices in the next room, female voices. Like a blind Peeping Tom, I pressed my ear to the door, but the wood was far too thick to allow me to discern their words. The conversation stopped. A door closed that I took to mean Janet had chosen a lady's maid from among the servants.

Potts came in with my freshly pressed shirt and collar. I asked him about the general tone below stairs.

"At Mrs. Frew's recommendation, Lady Pendry has chosen Mary to be her maid, sir. She's a bright girl, from what I see, and eager for the position. I hear they were friendly, her ladyship and the lass."

That made me smile. I was well aware of the chasm that separated the worlds above and below stairs. Towed to every social gathering as my mother's escort, I saw the staid arrangements in those households. Osgood and Fanny, paid servants though they were, watched over Mother and me with tender care that spoke of genuine regard far beyond their wages. I saw proof of it whenever their auras expanded in affection. In turn I was *very* fond of them. They were an essential part of my life from my earliest memory. Thinking on those auras, it occurred to me I'd seen the very same thing just a short while ago. Janet was held in deep affection by many at Carterhaugh, myself included. I smiled wistfully.

Potts helped me into my dinner jacket. Brushing the fabric free of lint, he said, "May I offer congratulations on your marriage, sir."

"Thank you, Potts. You are the only one to know we weren't wed three months past as gossip would have it. I'd keep it that way, if you take my meaning."

With a big smile he said assuredly, "I do recall it was a secret wedding, sir. Mid-August wasn't it?" With that, he turned and left me.

Chuckling, I checked my watch. Dinner here was still set to Uncle Charles's timepiece. It was now half past six. I was unsure if Janet had been told of the early dinner hour. Drawing a deep breath of resolve, I knocked on the door that separated our rooms. "Janet?"

The door opened on the loveliest of sights. Her moonlight hair was fashioned artfully high, no small feat that given the braided length swept halfway to the floor. Her attire was plain, but then she'd lived a much simpler life with her father. Dressing for dinner was likely not a part of their lives. I envisioned taking her on an excursion through London shops, picturing the light in her violet eyes as she sorted through fabrics and styles. The image brought about the sensation that my heart had expanded in my chest.

Quick as a flash, our ruse came to mind and I sobered. That daydream would never be. I had no need of these holdings. I'd be leaving before the weather turned, three to four weeks at best. I'd decided to leave a substantial purse behind as seed to start her on her birthright. The tenants would see to her financial keep beyond that. I offered her my arm. "May I escort you to dinner, Lady Pendry?"

She gave me a lovely smile and threaded her arm through mine. I led her through my room and down the stairs.

We soon discovered Mrs. Nevins had outdone herself with four courses and a superb eel pie. To my surprise, young Billy brought by a small cask of mead with my father-in-law's compliments. This Munro decanted for us. As my body was not yet past the numerous toasts to my good fortune the night before, I sipped prudently.

Janet was amiable dinner companionship. Careful of the footmen on hand, she shared the highlights of growing up in Selkirk, details that added color to all I'd guessed in the few exchanges we'd had. Her mind was sharp and inspective, and clearly the most intelligent female mind of my acquaintance. We laughed and teased and I warmed at the honest friendship developing between us.

Our goal was to intentionally make a display of ourselves for the benefit of the servants. Through an occasional show of affection, our hands would briefly touch. Twice I saw her shimmering rainbow-edged aura brighten as it had for her father and Billy. In my experience auras never lied. I had the distinct impression that perhaps she didn't find me odious after all. Foolish or not, it made me hopeful.

~*~

As it was expected whenever a laird takes a bride, Janet and I made the rounds through the village, kirk, and crofts over the course of several days. With the rare exception, the new Lady of Carterhaugh was well-received. There were a handful of people, however, who were less than welcoming. They didn't come to greet us but stayed behind their closed doors and peered through their windows.

Outwardly, Janet took this subtle prejudice in stride. I, on the other hand, took insult on her behalf. Janet deserved better as wife of the laird, charade or no. After the first wary encounter, I allowed Janet to determine where we'd venture next and made a mental note of those few homes we intentionally passed by. Making my silent inventory, I planned to knock on their doors another day. They would explain to me personally their prejudice. Thankfully, the wary were few and far between. I was genuinely warmed by those who more than made up for her poor reception by the few. Even MacPhee's superstitious Highland mother-in-law made a gracious greeting.

~*~

Under Rosie MacPhee's competent piloting, the planning committee saw to it that the harvest festival that weekend was a tremendous success. We'd had similar celebrations at Pendry, for we too had our tenants and renters. Yet I couldn't help but compare. Ours seemed a good deal stodgier than this lighthearted affair, but then again, I didn't have a beautiful bride on my arm at home.

On both sides of the border, estates of this size came with patrician duties rooted in tradition that went back centuries. The manor house and grounds of Pendry alone provided livelihood for fifty-two from Osgood to Pibbs, the gatekeeper. At home I was well aware of these responsibilities. In fact, I was born to the intricacies of caring for those people. I genuinely cared for the people here as well. At Janet's suggestion, I even filled my pockets with sweets for the children. All that was missing was the raven shatting down my back. Never before had I such a marvelous time executing my commitments.

~*~

Two weeks passed since Janet came to Carterhaugh as the laird's wife. According to Potts and Eppa, the story of us marrying in secret some months back was viewed as delightfully romantic. We added to the charade by letting it slip how we'd originally planned for her to come to me at Pendry. Our plans had changed when Uncle Charles passed away and I came to Carterhaugh instead. As our story went, we hadn't yet revealed all to her father but were waiting for an opportune time. It was that unpleasant business with Archie that necessitated we come clean. It helped that the headmaster told anyone who'd listen how pleased he was, despite the secrecy.

The tale certainly seemed plausible. A few well-placed morsels detailing our secret romance whenever servants were in earshot did the trick. In these moments, Janet's arm would wind through mine and our heads would tip toward one another as we continued, our talk seemingly oblivious to others in the vicinity. To the staff standing on hand at every turn, we surely appeared man and wife. I was the smitten bridegroom and took every opportunity to play my part. The marriage might be a sham, but lost in the depth of my feelings for this moonlit witch, I'd forget it.

Janet continued to treat various ills. I had a treatment room made up for her, adjacent to the herb beds, in the hope that at least some of her ambulatory patients would come here for her tinctures. It was a purely selfish act on my part, all to spend more time with her.

Weather agreeable, we'd walk the far corners of Carterhaugh; she for the ingredients used in her tinctures, and me for my ever-increasing catalogue of Lowland plant taxonomy. Away from our pretense, we came to know one another and a comfortable companionship developed between Janet and me. Whenever we came upon a flower, grass, or sedge on our outings, we'd exchange what we knew of it. She gave to me the common name and her use of it. I gave to her the Latin. Her innate intelligence and joyful nature made Janet enchanting company. Our excursions brought me indefinable happiness.

I found her a most singular woman. Though her birthright belonged to an aristocrat, that privileged life was never her experience. Through this unique perspective, she brought about in me a deeper understanding of the landlord/tenant symbiosis in the Scottish Lowlands. A clan chieftain once ruled these lands with tenants and banner men making a fighting force if necessary. Though no longer called to arms, the inclination for clan remained deeply rooted in the Scots. Fealty once given to the chieftain was now directed toward the laird. It certainly explained my earlier welcome.

September was now over and my time here was drawing to a close. With the accounting squared away and the various landlord obligations behind me, my departure was on the horizon and the handwriting on the wall. One day soon Janet would be both lady and landlord here and I would be gone from the lowlands. Though I longed to make her mine, I feared a second marriage proposal would ruin the friendship I'd come to cherish.

FOURTEEN

Mary hung the new dinner dress in the wardrobe and smoothed the fabric over the hanger. She turned to see Lady Janet unbraiding her hair at her dressing table. Unbound, the pale blond waves covered her like a shawl. Each night Mary offered to brush it for her and each time her lady declined. Mary offered again, "Are ye sure ye wouldn't want me t' help ye braid yer hair for bed?"

Janet smiled at the maid's reflection in the mirror and shook her head. "Thank you, no, Mary. I've been seeing to such things for most of my life."

"As ye wish, my lady. I'll be at hand whenever ye need me." With that, Mary bid her goodnight and left. Just as she was about to close the door behind her, the maid popped back around the door, and said sincerely, "If I may say so, Lady Janet, I think Laird Lenox is a fortunate man t' have ye."

"That's so nice of you to say. We both are."

Alone, Janet stared absently at her reflection in the glass, the truth of her last words echoing in her chest. The love light Billy spoke of existed; over the last three weeks, she'd seen a rainbow in the mirror whenever Lenox had come to mind. It was especially vibrant on their walks and sparkled and expanded on the edges of Lenox's aura each time they touched. Her own love light was now answering his.

She caught her reflection, smiling. She had fallen in love as quick and sure as any fae. And who wouldn't love him? Lenox was charming and witty, intelligent and kind, and every bit the laird he'd been raised to be. The thought made her pause. She wondered what magic had placed him in his father's own home.

The answer materialized: *Billy*. No one was kinder or more compassionate than the gentle hob. He'd been forced to commit a despicable act, but somehow, despite the queen's foul intentions, Billy had steered the course of Lenox's life by placing him with his father's own people. In effect, Lenox had been raised as the prince he was.

Hearing the deep rumble of male voices beyond the door, Janet put aside her brush and listened. Lenox was speaking with his man. The rumble turned to silence, followed by the sound of a door closing.

On impulse, she went to the door that separated her bedroom from his and rapped lightly. Unsure if he'd heard her knock, she put her ear to the wood and listened. The door suddenly swung open into Lenox's room. Janet squeaked in surprise as she tumbled headlong over the threshold to collide with his chest. He held her in his arms to steady her and laughter danced in the air. Their eyes met as they straightened. The words she intended to speak evaporated when his hand glided from her bare arm to the back of her neck. The other swept around her waist to gently pull her close. He kissed her then, softly asking permission for more.

And more was exactly what she wanted. Her arms wound around him and she pressed her body against his. Lips parted in an ever deepening kiss that made her dizzy with want. He blazed a path of kisses over her face and down the column of her neck. When he swept her up into his arms to carry her to his bed, she kissed him again.

~*~

Munro came to me at breakfast with a note from Janet saying the babe was not yet born. My moonlit witch was called away at a most inopportune moment the night before, when a young lad pounded on the kitchen door at midnight, crying that his mother labored hard to deliver her baby.

Nevertheless, a threshold had been crossed last night, literally and figuratively. I'd felt her aura pulsing at the door that separated our rooms and when I opened it, she tumbled into my arms. Even something so small and simple as Janet's hand in mine sent a thrill coursing up my arm. Holding her body against mine defied description. I felt electrified. There was naught to do but kiss her. To my joy she returned it with a hunger that matched my own. Though no formal union existed between us, the charade of wedded bliss felt true. I wasn't sure how much time passed as we stood wrapped in one another's arms, sharing kisses that made my soul complete, but I knew she felt the same. For when I took her in my arms to carry her to my bed to make love to her, she kissed me with such passion I thought surely my heart would burst.

We'd no sooner shed our clothes when came the unfortunate knock upon her door. I offered to take her to the village but she declined, saying her horse overland was faster.

I lay awake some hours fairly overcome with happiness. I knew in my heart my moonlit witch loved me. It was all I could do not to shout my happiness from the rooftops. When I did manage to sleep, I did so with my senses fully aroused. Body and soul, I ached with the want of her. I wanted to hold her, to kiss her, to again feel her bare body against mine. More than anything, I wished to surrender to that rainbow that wrapped around me and made me whole. No longer fearing rejection, I'd ask her to marry me the moment she returned.

Her note said she'd be gone several hours more. I looked out the window, hoping for some miracle that would see Janet riding up the drive. Anxious for her return, I heard myself sigh. The morning sun was shining and I the besotted fool was getting worse by the second. Welcoming a distraction, I called for Potts to assemble my gear.

~*~

This first week of October was quite warm but just yesterday morning I'd felt the change in the air. Winter would settle on these Scottish lands before long. I pictured snow on these picturesque hills. Would we stay the winter or return to Pendry? Last night's intimacy had charted a new course for our lives. We had much to discuss.

I hadn't a purpose or direction in mind when I set out, but found myself in the derelict Roxburgh gardens. The flowers of the season, like the Lowland summer, were spent now. Surprised, I spied one remnant bloom among the withered roses. I ran my fingertip over a pink petal and smiled. Janet's skin was soft like this. Deciding to present it along with my proposal, I packed it among the moss in my vasculum for safe keeping.

Walking on, I soon came to the bow in the stream where a downed willow hugged the bank. Archie had plotted his foul deed here, and I felt a prickling of ire at the memory. The sound of splashing water drew my attention. Sensing Janet's presence, my elated heart began to pound. I peered over the top of the fallen trunk. She *was* here and as beautifully bare as a naiad. Her horse lifted its head to look at me and then returned to grazing without making a sound. On impulse, I stripped to my skin and silently waded her way. She must have sensed me as well, for she turned in all her porcelain glory and treated me to a beauteous smile.

I found my voice. "All is well with the mother, I take it?"

"Yes. I helped see a strapping boy of *considerable* size into the world."

I made my way closer. Lord, the water was cold the deeper in. I told her so, adding, "If only I had my net. What a catch you'd make."

She laughed and continued bathing. Face washed, she swept her damp hair back and tucked it behind her ears. How extraordinary. There was no one else of my acquaintance with somewhat pointy ears, a physical trait I'd long associated with my deceased father. I wondered if it was a trick of light upon the water. Desiring a closer look, I stepped in her direction and a sharp stab of unimaginable pain raced from my instep up the whole of my body. I fell into the water with a howl. A plume of red colored the water around me.

Janet splashed her way to my side. "Lenox! What is it? What's the matter?"

I couldn't yet find my voice, the pain taking my next breath completely.

"Here." She put my arm over her shoulder. I leaned against her and lifted my foot. Sticking through the top of my foot was the forked tine of a rusted iron fishing gig. Janet gasped, her expression horrified. She steered me to shore and said urgently, "We need to see to that immediately!"

Together we struggled on three legs, but unbalanced as I was, my good foot slipped on the muddy bank. We fell on the ground and when I stumbled and the tine piercing my foot busted on impact. All I could do was roll in a knot of agony.

The sound of rummaging could be heard behind me and I assumed Janet was searching through her healer's valise. A moment later, she was sitting on my leg. She tossed over her shoulder, "This will hurt, Lenox, but you must bear it regardless. Do you understand? I must get that iron fragment out as quickly as possible."

Her words sounded far away. A searing pain exploded in my brain and my body twisted to escape the torment. I realized she was cutting into me with her knife.

"Hold *still*, Lenox!" Janet thundered. She renewed her efforts.

Anguish ran up my leg like fire. I felt very strange. I could hear myself asking her to stop but my lips didn't move. Worse, the world was going pale; the color of it draining away like paint box temperas left in the rain.

"Damn it all, Lenox, you will *not* die!"

Was I dying? There were too many things I'd yet to do, to die. Too many things left unsaid. I thought I heard my voice again, but I wasn't certain. My pale world went black.

~*~

Frantic, Janet ran for her kit and rummaged for her silver herb knife. Lodged between the bones in Lenox's ankle was a small piece of a rusted fishing gig. If she didn't get the fragment out of his body, the iron would kill his fae blood. She straddled his legs and sat, pinning him under her. Knife in hand, she sunk the tip of her silver blade deeper into the wound and felt the coarse scrape as her knife made contact. Try as she might to dig the fragment free, it wouldn't budge. Heart wrenching shudders of pain vibrated under her, then Lenox suddenly stilled. She whirled around to find him unconscious. Pressing her fingers hard into his groin, she felt for a pulse — erratic but still strong. Thank the goddess for that.

Now that he was oblivious to the pain, she redoubled her efforts. Time and again she felt the catch of rusty iron against the silver knife edge, but she couldn't see beyond the pooling blood that blocked her view as quickly as she blotted it away. Surrendering to the fact that there was nothing else to do, she bound the wound as tightly as she dared. His skin was going cold. She quickly donned her chemisette and pantalets then covered Lenox with the rest of her clothing.

Searching the sky, she spied a lark and whistled, as Billy taught her. Holding out a finger for the bird to land, she told him, "Bring Billy and Papa and a cart. Tell them Lenox is injured and I'm afraid he'll die. Please hurry, little friend."

~*~

Knitting socks at the hearth, Billy was surprised to hear a lark tapping on the window. He opened the sash and the bird flew inside. The hob's eyes grew wide and fearful upon hearing what the bird had to say. Shoving the plate of crumbs left from his tea before the lark, he said, "For your good deed, my dear. Eat quickly, for you must lead us there."

Billy transformed into the boy and hurried to Eppa's classroom, where he waved wildly from the back of the room to get headmaster's attention.

Eppa closed his book and checked his watch. He told his students, "Gather your belongings, children. That is all for today. Read your Bullfinch tonight — chapter thirteen. We will discuss the lives of Echo and Narcissus when we gather next. I shall see you bright and early tomorrow morning."

Alone now, Eppa turned to Billy, who relayed the news from the lark.

Having gathered what they needed, they followed the bird but abandoned the horse and wagon when the road ended. Hurrying after the anxious lark on foot, they crossed to the Roxburgh side of the stream and found Janet cradling an unconscious Lenox. Both were covered in blood and it was obvious Lenox had been touched by death.

Janet looked up at them with red-rimmed eyes and sobbed, "I — I feel him *dying*, Papa."

Eppa rushed forward. "My darling girl, *what* has happened here?"

Her voice a defeated whisper, she tipped her head to the rusted broken metal lying beside her silver knife and explained all, adding through her tears, "The tine snapped when he fell. A small piece is lodged . . . lodged between the ankle bones. I can't remove it."

Clearly distraught, Billy was phasing from one form to another to a combination thereof. He said, "Oh the iron…it kills. We cannot allow that! We must get it out out out!"

Lenox groaned.

Eppa stripped his coat and vest and wrapped them around Lenox before unwrapping the foot to assess the wound. Fresh bleeding followed. He said, "Find spider webs, Billy, a dozen at the least. More would be better." To Janet, he said, "Is there tincture of poppy in your bag, and yarrow?"

She nodded.

"Bring them, quickly."

Billy and Janet scattered in opposite directions and returned moments later. A large yellow spider sat on Billy's shoulder and a smaller black one clung to his shirt front, but his spindly fingers were draped in orb weaver webs.

Cradling Lenox's head again, Janet carefully dribbled her poppy tincture into his mouth.

Searching the ground for a fist-sized cobble, Eppa found a likely stone and told his daughter, "Put all your weight on his leg, just here. Do not let him move." Janet hurried to do as instructed.

With the silver knife point hard up against the iron fragment, Eppa grasped the stone and with it gave the knife handle a hard *whack*. Lenox moaned as the bone fractured, and then he arched his back and fell unconscious once more, as the iron came free. There was nothing Eppa could do about the iron rust already tainting Lenox's blood. Eppa sprinkled the powdered yarrow over the wound to stanch the blood flow then motioned for Billy to bring the spider webs. The healing properties of spider silk would help regenerate the torn flesh.

Billy said, "I've found twenty-four, but see three more just over there." He pointed with a web-covered finger. "I'll get those too."

Eppa laid the first web over the wound. Gently wielding the tip of the silver knife, he eased the sticky silk between the white ligaments, getting as close to the broken bone as he could. He then covered the punctures with webs and more bandages. There was nothing else to be done. Iron was a dangerous thing to their kind, deadly even to the half-bloods if it somehow entered the marrow, and it had. The iron was now poisoning Lenox. Their only hope lay in the fact that rust was by definition decaying. By nature, rust made the killing properties of iron weaker. Eppa met his daughter's eye and offered the only hope he had. "I've seen the effects of rusted iron before. Lenox will have a high fever and delirium before his work is done. Should he survive it, his body will sweat the iron out when the fever breaks. If he manages to pull through, he will be weak for some time."

"I'm afraid, Papa." Janet fought back her tears.

Eppa gathered her into his arms, his next words echoing her unspoken emotion. "You do love him, then." He felt the nod against his chest. "I won't hide the truth from you, my dearest. His next hours will be precarious. You need to understand this — Lenox will survive this infection or he won't. Should he die, it will *not* be of *your* doing. His fae blood only has a chance if the human part of him fights to live. Tend to him, care for him, and every step of the way convey that you love him. I suspect were he to know of your love he'd fight hell itself to return to you."

Billy's arms were filled with Lenox's clothing and things. Together they dressed him quickly and managed to get him into the cart with the help of Billy's magic.

Billy told Janet as she dressed, "I will send you more spider webs, Janet dear. Watch for a raven to bring them." Before she could thank him, he ran off toward the meadow where large orb weaver webs shimmered in the sun.

Turning to her father, she said, "Thank you, Papa. I'll send word." Leaving her horse for them, she clucked her tongue at the carriage horse and sped to Carterhaugh.

~*~

Mrs. Nevins nudged her way through the throng, having been called away from her baking by her grandson. He'd brought terrible news: Laird Lenox had been seriously injured. Every person in the household crammed the narrow hallway as tightly as a box of salted cod. The cook made her way to the front to see the unconscious young master being carried up the stairs by Potts and her eldest son, Burley. Lady Janet hurried up the stairs after them, her own clothing covered in blood. The cook gasped, "Good heavens!" Tugging the housekeeper's shawl, she asked, "Glynnis, how did this happen?"

Mrs. Frew shook her head. "There wasna time t' ask her ladyship th' whys an' wherefores. Master Lenox has been injured, only tha' much I *do* know."

"But all tha' blood…"

Standing near, Munro said, "It appears to belong t' his lairdship. Fer now, we wait on Lady Janet t' make her needs known. She'll decide to explain it or no."

Mrs. Nevins said, "If his lairdship is in a bad way, Mr. Munro, I doubt she'd take her supper. I'll put some broth on straightaway."

"Aye, Hester. Something nourishing, it's bound t' be a verra long night."

On a mission, the cook spun on her heel and nudged her way back through the crowd. She snapped at the footmen and maids, her children mostly, "Och, go about yer business now. There's no need fer ye all t' be standing here with yer mouths open like trout. Go on, off w' ye."

Left alone in the hall with the housekeeper, Munro told Mrs. Frew, "Potts said he was takin' one o' his walks fer th' plants he collects. I wonder where

Lady Janet found him."

"I can't imagine. She was midwifing the Reynold's newest bairn, last anyone knew."

"Do ye think it wise t' call fer the doctor? I can send young Boyd."

Mrs. Frew's instinct said whatever it was, it was fae business. She said, "Lady Janet is a healer, there's no better hands fer the young master to be in than hers."

FIFTEEN

The litter bearers headed for the master bedroom. Needing the afternoon light the two walls of windows would provide in her corner room, Janet directed they bring Lenox there instead. In the secretary, she found two sheets of paper and pen and quickly scribbled down her immediate needs. To the footman, she handed one sheet and explained, "Burley, please take this message to Mr. Munro. I'll need these things seen to right away." She handed him the other, adding, "And please see this list goes to Mrs. Frew."

"Yes, Lady Janet. I'll see t' it."

To Lenox's worried manservant, Janet said, "Your master has poisoned himself on rusted metal."

Potts cast a horrified eye on the pale bloodstained body of his master lying on the bed. "Is it the lockjaw, ma'am?"

"Lockjaw." Janet repeated dully. Would his human blood be tainted with that killing infection while his fae half fought the iron in his blood? Fear twisting her insides, she shook her head. "I can't think about that right now. I don't yet know if he can survive the iron in his blood." Ignoring the man's look of confusion, she said, "I'll need your help to get him undressed, but do not disturb his foot. Cut away his clothing if necessary."

They soon had Lenox unclothed and tucked warmly under several quilts with his injured foot sitting high on pillows to slow the swelling. An out of breath Winnet panted in the doorway, "Excuse me, Lady Janet, I've bought th' first item's ye called fer. Mary is working with Mrs. Nevin and Mrs. Frew right now t' get th' rest together."

Burley returned with bundled lengths of smooth branches that had their bark removed. "I've brought ye th' splints ye asked fer, Lady Janet. Mr. Ennis sent several lengths an' says be sure t' tell ye he took them down with his draw knife, so they're smooth. He can make them smoother still, if ye need them so."

Janet ran a hand over the wood and found them perfectly smooth. "Thank you, Burley, and please give Mr. Ennis my appreciation as well."

Mary and her twin brother Arnold came with a tray filled with bowls and herbs and an armload of logs for the hearth. Feeling Lenox's forehead, Janet said, "Arnold, do get that fire started straightaway, and Winnet, light a fire in the grate as well. He's taken a chill. I need this room warmed quickly."

A flurry of activity saw the fires lit and the table set with herbs, bandages, and tools. Munro watched from the doorway, his obvious concern lowering his bushy brows. Needing to think without distraction, Janet thanked them all and then asked them to leave.

Clearly in turmoil, Potts didn't move. Munro said gently, "Come away, Mr. Potts."

Feeling genuine concern emanating off the manservant, Janet turned to Potts, and said to the head butler, "I'll need Potts a while longer, Mr. Munro."

"Aye, as ye wish, Lady Janet."

Alone with the manservant, she said matter-of-factly, "You're fond of my husband."

"I am, ma'am. My family has served his for more than one hundred years. His lordship is a fine man."

She dipped a small towel in her bowl of hot water and astringent herbs and gently washed Lenox's face and neck. Uncovering a portion of his body at a time so as not to chill him further, she wiped him down.

"Ma'am?"

"Yes, Potts?"

"Will he . . . ?"

Reading his unspoken anxiety, she told him gently, "I don't know, but rest assured I will do my best for him. Do keep us both in your thoughts. Go now and find yourself a cup of tea. I shall call on you if necessary."

"Yes, ma'am." Potts bowed his head, then turned and left the room.

~*~

Lenox's wounds were growing angry and red, despite Eppa's application of antiseptic spider silk. Thankfully Janet's patient didn't rouse when she removed the bandages, inspiring fresh blood to spill. The edges of torn flesh were scabbing but a purplish discoloration had begun under the skin and appeared to be spreading over the top of the rapidly swelling foot. She felt his skin again. He was still too cold to the touch. Worse, his aura was weaker now.

A knock at the door sounded before it opened. Janet turned to find Mrs. Frew with a jar in hand. The housekeeper said, "Young Boyd and his brother Simon found ye some leeches like ye wanted."

"Thank you —" Janet said, reaching out a hand when she interrupted by a light tapping at the window. She knew it was Billy's envoy with the spider webs he'd promised. Not wanting to reveal her helper bird, Janet ignored it. The bird tapped again, harder and more insistent this time.

Mrs. Frew said, "Janet dear, *Lady* Janet. I've known what ye are since th' night ye were born right here in this bed. Yer secret is safe wi' me, as it always has been." Looking at her over the top of her spectacles, she added, "Just as yer father's secret is safe, safe as the secret I hold for this young man here." She tipped her head toward Lenox on the bed.

Stunned at the admission, Janet didn't know how to respond.

Smiling gently, the housekeeper patted her arm and nodded. "Aye, I know it, even if his lairdship has no idea."

The bird rapped again.

"*Dear* Mrs. Frew." With a small whimper, Janet hugged the old woman tightly before rushing to the window to open the sash. A raven hopped forward to deposit a bundled bit of cloth into her waiting hand. She thanked him quickly then closed the window, lest another member of the household enter the room to see a raven acting so peculiar. Folding back the corners of the handkerchief she discovered more spider webs.

Looking from the handkerchief to the lady of the manor, Mrs. Frew's brows drew together. "Ye have a need fer spider's webs?"

Janet nodded. "To keep infection at bay."

The housekeeper shook her head in wonder. "Imagine that."

~*~

Glynnis Frew watched the healer skillfully treat the young master's wounds. Lady Janet was calm but there was deep anxiety shining in those violet-blue eyes. Only twice did Laird Lenox stir, and no wonder, with his wife pushing spider webs inside his flesh with the tip of a small silver knife. The same knife tip was then heated in a candle flame and pressed to his flesh to cauterize the wound, which stubbornly refused to stop bleeding.

When she asked what caused the wound, Lady Janet explained, and said the greater danger was iron contaminating the blood. She further explained the iron is deadly to fae, even to the half-blooded. Glynnis's mind reeled. Wee Owen once scratched himself on a rusty nail and death hovered over his bed for a week. Now she knew the *iron* was why. She briefly explained her changeling cousin from long ago and his experience with iron, to let the poor worried lass know he'd lived, despite the high fever and no one knowing the cause of his illness. She asked, "Can ye touch iron, then?"

Janet nodded. "Yes, and I can cook in iron pots as well. But iron entering the body poisons the blood if too much time passes. A piece of the rusted tine broke off inside Lenox's ankle bone."

Glynnis put both hands to her cheeks. "Oh my goodness, the poor laddie."

Janet set the leeches on the swollen areas above and below the exit and entry wounds. They drank their fill and before long were the size of quail eggs. As they filled and could take no more, they fell away from the skin one by one. Putting three back in the jar, Glynnis said, "I'll take th' wee beasties. Th' laddies can dump them back in th' pond."

Grabbing a bloated leech before it stained the linen, Janet dropped it in the jar, but shook her head. "The little creatures have given their lives, Mrs. Frew. They've taken the poison into themselves and have died from it. Burn them or bury them where no animal will chance upon them."

"Ah, I see." Glynnis said, picking two more off the floor. When the last dropped away, she asked, "The poison is out then, so his lairdship is in th' clear?"

"No. His condition will — " Choking up, Janet cleared her throat but her words came out broken, "He will take a turn. Of that much I am certain." She swallowed hard. "The truth is he may not survive it."

Glynnis set the jar aside and gathered the poor motherless lass in her arms to hold her while she cried. "Come dear, cry it out. There, there. He's a strong braw laddie. And yer healing touch is such a gift. If anyone can help his lairdship, it's you, dear."

~*~

The glass orb came rolling into the great hall. Oonagh picked it up and held it to her ear. The echo of her changeling's voice spoke softly:

Mother,

I followed Aunt to a place called Pendry. There she spoke with a woman and took a horse. The woman told aunt she would follow in a fortnight and said, "Please make certain Lenox is not hurt in all of this." To that, Aunt replied, "I would die before I brought him pain." This was all I was able to hear. I was unable to discover who this Lenox is. I am very sorry, Mother.

Enraged over the implication, Oonagh shrieked.

Her hand squeezed tight in her anger, the orb shattering under the pressure. She didn't hear the gasps of the courtiers nor did she realize the glass shards had cut her hand. The only thing on her mind was dragging her sister's son to hell. As blood ran down her wrist, she envisioned spilling Rowan's blood — the feckless human. And Orlaith would be there to see both changelings die.

SIXTEEN

If anything declared Lenox part fae it was his rapid healing. The punctures were completely healed over after only two days. If not for the purplish discoloration that ran nearly the full length of his leg, Janet would have been pleased. The iron poisoning was spreading. She felt his bare thigh and found his skin very cold to the touch, as cold as death. Fever alone had the power to sweat the contaminant out of his blood. She knew her lack of rest was beginning to cloud her mind. She wracked her brain for a solution, but the answer was beyond her grasp.

A light rap at the door was followed by creaky opening. Mrs. Frew's head peeked around the corner. "I've brought ye some broth and a nice warm bannock with butter, Lady Janet."

"Thank you Mrs. Frew, but I'm not hungry at this moment. Please, set it over there."

The housekeeper looked at the uneaten breakfast on the table and tsked. "It is because of our past together that I shall speak plainly, an' I hope ye forgive me fer it," she said. "Yer looking weary an' low, dear. I'll wager ye have no' slept a wink these last two nights. I *know* yer not eating."

Janet let out a weary breath. "No, I haven't done much of either."

The housekeeper said, "Now I'm no' a healer, an' my understanding of th' auld ways is sparse, but I do know *work*. A body can no' work effectively beaten down by lack of sleep an' taking no' meals. Perhaps ye'd have a bath an' eat a bit, just t' refresh yerself. Take a wee nap even. I can sit watch on his lairdship while ye do. There's no' much to it while he sleeps, is there?" She smiled encouragingly and patted her large apron pocket. With an air of premeditated cunning, she added, "An' I've brought my embroidery for such an instance."

Janet rubbed her weary eyes. Mrs. Frew was right. She'd been worried if she dared look away for a moment, Lenox's condition would turn. As a result, her thoughts were everywhere at once and useful to none. The worst was yet to come, so she'd better rest now. Conceding to the elder's judgment, Janet said appreciatively, "You're a wise woman, Glynnis Frew."

The broth and buttery bannock were both delicious. Feeling much improved, Janet quickly went to bathe. She briefly considered napping in the chair beside Lenox, but Mrs. Frew convinced her to seek a sounder restorative sleep in the laird's chambers. There on Lenox's bed, with his comforting scent surrounding her, she fell into a deep exhausted sleep.

~*~

A pain-studded howl followed by the sounds of shuffling and low voices woke Janet from her nap. She bolted from the bed and ran toward the scuffle. There she found Mrs. Frew looking blue around the lips and clutching her chest, and Potts struggling to hold a writhing Lenox down on the bed. Noting the housekeeper's immediate need, Janet ran to her medicinal bag and rummaged through the assorted jars and pouches. She mixed several of them into an empty teacup, thrust it into the hands of the housekeeper, and said emphatically, "Sit and drink this, this instant."

Mrs. Frew drank the tonic with a wrinkled nose. Her face and aura instantly took on a healthy glow. The housekeeper drew a deep breath, and said, "I'm fine now, Lady Janet, only too much excitement. It's a guid thing Mr. Potts was checking on his lairdship just now. It was all I could to keep him on th' bed when the writhing started."

"Yes, it was most assuredly a good thing." Satisfied with the elder's instant improvement, Janet turned her attention toward Lenox and the manservant struggling to keep him on the bed. She hurried to her bureau to fetch her stockings.

Voice cracking, Potts looked at her helplessly over his shoulder, his eyes wide with fear. "It's the lockjaw, ma'am, he's having terrible spasms. Oh my poor sir, my *poor* sir."

Unable to assure him it wasn't lockjaw without explaining what Lenox was, she said, "We'll need to tie him down so he doesn't hurt himself." Using the stockings, they tied his wrists and his uninjured ankle to the bedstead, with Potts gaining a bloody nose for his trouble.

Handing the manservant a pad of linen, Janet said, "I am so sorry for that. Pinch your nose, that's right, just there. Thank you for your timely assistance, Potts. You may go. "

"But ma'am, his lordship is a strong man. I'd not see him inadvertently do *this* to *you*." He pulled the scarlet pad away from his face just long enough to illustrate his injury.

Teeth clenched in a grimace of pain, Lenox growled as another spasm arched his back from the bed. Potts choked on fear-laced words, "I know he'd prefer it ma'am. He'd prefer me to protect you from *him*, if necessary."

"I appreciate your concern and I thank you for it, but he'll not harm me tied as he is. If you would, I'd like you to escort Mrs. Frew to her rooms. The medicine will soon make her very tired." To the housekeeper she said, "The tincture was a strong one, you'd best lie down. I'll not have you fainting on the stairs."

"Och dear, dinna ye worry about me. But yes, I am a wee bit tired from it." To Potts she added, "Come laddie. Let us leave her ladyship in peace."

Janet said, "Thank you both."

At the door, Mrs. Frew turned. "Shall I'll send ye a maid to put the room t' rights, Lady Janet?"

Lenox arched and groaned. Potts looked stricken. Janet shook her head. "Not right now, Mrs. Frew. I'll ring if I need further assistance."

~*~

Eppa found Billy in the stable conversing with Janet's goat while he milked her. Amid warm squirts into the pail and the meows of a stray cat, he heard Billy say, "Warmer her hands may be, my dear, but Janet isn't here and I must get the milking done. You have no kid to suckle and if I don't you will soon grow full and sore. Janet wouldn't want that to happen."

The goat gave a bleat of admonishment followed with a head toss that nearly toppled the hob from his milking stool. Eppa bit back a chuckle. He might not understand the language of animals directly as Billy did, but he certainly understood the message.

Billy clucked his tongue in admonishment, "There now, no need for that. I *swear* I'll warm my hands by the fire before the next milking."

The goat let out a long corrugated bleat.

"Yes, I miss her too. Yes, I realize she hasn't come to visit this week, but the young prince needs her care. You must understand her home is elsewhere now." He finished with a cup of oats in the trough and a splash of milk in a pan for the cat. The horse's nicker must have alerted Billy to Eppa's presence, for he spoke before turning. "I was just tending our friends. They miss your daughter."

The animals' auras dimmed as they shared their thoughts with the gentle hob. Eppa hadn't missed their sadness, nor had he missed Billy's unspoken words. In his short time here, Billy had grown to love Janet. They all keenly felt her absence.

He took the full bucket of milk from Billy's hand, and asked, "Has Janet sent word of Lenox's condition?"

Billy shook his head, "Not a word nor a bird."

"This is the third day." Eppa reminded him, "Tonight will see the worst of it."

~*~

A soft thud hit the window pane. Billy hurried there and opened the sash. He looked around and discovered a small snow bunting, an exhausted bird by the look of him. He cradled the limp creature in his hands.

Eppa asked, "Did Janet send him?"

"I'm not sure. He's far too weary to tell me. Please keep our little friend warm, I'll only be a moment." Before depositing the bird into Eppa's warm hands, he told it softly, "Rest now, my dear. Water and worms will see you quickly restored."

Raising his glamour in a sparkling swirl, Billy transformed into the boy and went to find earthworms under the stones in the yard. Returning several minutes later with several wriggling in his grimy hand, he coaxed the bird to eat and drink, then allowed him a few minutes of post-meal preening to settle his full crop. He then asked the bird why he had come.

Eppa listened to the exchange, unable to understand the bird's chatter. "What is it Billy, is it Lenox? Has he taken a turn?"

Billy broke unto a vibrant smile and sparkled with happiness. He said, "No my friend, this is very *good* news, yes yes yes, it is!" He jumped up and started tidying his yarn basket and knitting needles.

Eppa looked at him expectantly, but Billy wasn't forthright in sharing the bird's message. In fact, he looked like he was trying hard to keep his happy secret.

"Billy!"

Excited, Billy suddenly blurted, "The bunting says she's but an hour away, but we must take into account he speaks of time and distance as a bird flies."

"Who?"

"Our dear Orlaith comes here!"

Eppa could hardly believe his ears. Orlaith would never leave the Aos Sidhe. He shared that opinion.

Billy asked the bird if he knew more. The bunting flew to Billy's finger then chipped and chattered and ended in a loud impatient tweet. In a flash, he returned to the mantelpiece and there continued on with his preening. Billy nodded. "Yes, such a trip *does* ruffle one's feathers. Thank you for this happy news, little friend."

Eppa raised his silvery brows. "Well?"

"She received my note asking her to come. She rides this way and will arrive midday."

"A note? When did you send a note?"

"When I first set eyes upon the young prince."

"Why?"

"To right a wrong." His large brown eyes misting with tears, Billy changed into his natural form. Glamour was difficult to maintain when emotions were high. He explained, "Oonagh's mind was set against Orlaith's child before he was even born. I knew she would have killed the babe had I not done this terrible thing, just as she murdered poor King Ruaraidh and my precious Maeve. I took him away that he might live, but it's time to give Lenox back to his mother. I need to right the wrong I was forced to do. I've already done as much as I might for the other lad."

"What have you done for Rowan?"

A large handkerchief appeared out of nowhere. Billy snuffled into it before admitting, "I gave Rowan a charm to remove the lie from his life."

Eppa listened. He didn't know the man Rowan had become, only knew the very disagreeable child he had been. Having been raised in Oonagh's image, Rowan was a boy people tended to keep at arm's length. As a lamb for slated slaughter, Oonagh set him apart on purpose. It was heartbreaking for all who knew and could do nothing to change it. Doubtful, Eppa asked Billy if the charm would be strong enough to break the enchantment of *The Black Opus*.

"This time it is." Billy nodded.

"You've tried before?"

"*Many* times and never did my efforts succeed. But I recently I realized I'd gone about it the wrong way. I was working large magic when I should have worked small."

"*The Black Opus* would need large magic to counter it, no?"

Billy explained, "You would think so, wouldn't you? But no, the mind who conceived such a terrible thing made it impervious to strong magic. That's what makes the book unimaginably deadly. There is no way to counter charm of *The Black Opus* itself."

Billy shared all the ways he had tried to dissolve the charm on Rowan, and how many times — dozens of times — Oonagh came close to discovering his meddling. Eppa shook his head in wonder. How brave of Billy. As insane as Oonagh was, she would have killed him had she known. It would have been a slow killing too.

Billy said, "By giving Rowan a small gift of doubt it does not come in contact with the dark charm at all. It simply helps him see and the rest is up to him. Every day things will occur that do not matter, small things of no interest or importance to Oonagh, but his mind will see through the enchantment just long enough to see each one and question why they are the way they are. Each time his mind fills with doubt, the doubt becomes stronger. It will eventually remove the blind acceptance from his heart and when it does, he will flee the Aos Sidhe."

"That's brilliant, Billy. I hope Rowan's doubt frees him soon. Samhain approaches."

"It will. I took from my own life to ensure it."

"Billy, *no.*" Shortly after Billy arrived in Selkirk, he'd shared what brought about the king's and queen's deaths. Had the hob not intervened with the strength of his own life essence, Oonagh would have murdered Orlaith as well. And now he had sacrificed more of his life for Rowan.

Billy held up a spindly-fingered hand. "*None* of this was Rowan's doing, Eppa. He'll soon turn twenty-five and he must be well away from Oonagh before then. I must make amends for the part I played. Understand this was necessary, my friend. I know all too well the strength of the dark enchantments in that accursed book." Growing emotion made his nose run. He honked wetly into his handkerchief then went to tidy the bookshelves.

Eppa told him sincerely, "You have a good heart, my friend."

Eppa well understood the weight of guilt the hob lived with over Lenox and Rowan, for he lived with guilt of his own. All those years ago he'd been compelled to murder Oonagh's man, lest he reveal young Lenox's whereabouts. His soul still wept for the deed but he knew he would do it again to protect Orlaith, and now she was on her way here. He felt as if his happy heart would burst. This time he would tell her of his love without her stepsister barring his way. Goddess willing, after all these years she would feel the same. A damp rag hit him on the forehead and burst the bubble of his daydream.

Billy chided him. "With Janet gone, just look at this house. Orlaith will think you live in a sty, my friend."

Eppa chuckled. To Billy a spare crumb was too large a mess. Hobs were consummate housekeepers and nothing made them happier than a tidy home. His friend's mood was obviously lifted by this happy task. Picking the damp cloth off his shirt front, Eppa tidied the already immaculate little house, his heart dancing in anticipation.

~*~

From his hiding place behind the shed, Rowan watched the red-haired young woman take two younger children in hand. She called out, "Peter!"

He didn't see the older woman from this vantage point. Libby, her husband had called her, but heard her say, "Ye'd best hurry, Peter. Mr. Gallager's countin' on us t' get his apples picked."

An older boy, Peter presumably, ran to catch up, a stack of empty bushel baskets jumbled awkwardly in his arms. He called after them, "Bessie…wait!"

He heard Libby laugh and then she began to sing to herself. An odd sensation passed over him. Rowan started to tremble. He didn't know why, but he'd been compelled to come to this place. And now he was inspired to speak with this woman despite having nothing in mind to say. He stepped from behind the shed and headed toward the sound of her voice. He found her with back to him busily hanging newly washed clothing to dry. He opened his mouth to speak, but no sound came forth. He tried again. Nothing. In a panic, he spun on his heel and ran to the under hill.

~*~

Struck by the sudden sensation she wasn't alone, Libby scanned the yard. Seeing no one, she shrugged. "Yer imaginin' things, Libby old girl."

She glanced at the tree in the corner of their stable yard. This year it was so full of orange-red berries that the branches were sagging under the weight. Danny had planted that rowan tree over the grave of their son Albert, who they'd lost nearly twenty-five years before. The tree was precious to her and she'd hate to lose it. She'd have Peter take a rake to it to knock the berry clusters from the worrisome limbs.

Thinking of Albert, she wondered what her son would have looked like had he lived. All their boys and the eldest girl took after their father's side in face and build, and all but two in coloring. For some reason that ginger-haired young man they'd met in the village came to mind. Inexplicably, she began to weep.

~*~

Rowan ran to the Aos Sidhe. At the side of the hill, where the ancient yew tree stood, he searched for the faint silver line that hid this world from the other. Pushing past the barrier, he stepped inside. He eyed his private doorway, an entrance made just for him by Mother. For years he'd believed his doorway was special because he was the prince, but now he wondered why he was unable to enter anywhere else. For the third time an odd sensation passed over him and this time he knew it by name. *Doubt*

.

SEVENTEEN

Lenox's turn for the worse was far beyond Janet's experience. His human half had yet to bring on the fever that his fae half needed to fight the blood poisoning. The contamination triggered terrible muscle spasms, the result of once healthy fae blood dying in his veins. Pain contorted his body. Delirium followed.

Writhing in pain, Lenox cried out and mumbled unintelligibly in turns. At one point, it sounded as though he were reliving an angry encounter with Archie MacGilliveray. But mostly he called for Janet, at times weeping her name in his misery. Billy was right. Length of acquaintance did not matter. Their kind did know when love touched them, and Lenox Pendry touched Janet's heart as no one ever had.

Struggling against the spasms, she managed to dose him with poppy tincture. Even in sleep the terrible spasms made him grimace and moan. She caressed him as he calmed and told him repeatedly that she loved him.

Despite the exertion, his skin was still cold and dry. She added more wood to the fire and the room grew so warm that sweat tickled between her breasts. She unfastened another button and brushed her damp hair back from her face. External heat wasn't helping. It wasn't making *him* sweat.

She paced the room, seeking inspiration. Since answering a healer's calling at age fourteen, she'd treated many fevers but never once started one. *A diaphoretic!* An idea suddenly took her and she flew to the tabletop. There she sorted through jars and bottles and garden herbs from the kitchen. *Mullen, no. Eyebright, no. Boneset! Yes, boneset will bring about sweating. And ginger, lots of ginger.*

She found two more plants with diaphoretic properties and mixed the boneset, pennyroyal, cayenne, and ginger together. Dipping her fingertip to taste, she winced at the spicy after burn it left on her tongue.

Cradling his head, she said, "Lenox, I've a tonic for you. Lenox, dearest?"

He remained unresponsive. She gently shook him. He moaned but didn't stir. Leaning close, she spoke at his ear, "*Please*. You *need* this." She opened his mouth and administered a few drops off the tip of a silver spoon. Most dribbled out. She dabbed his chin and urged him on. After several attempts, she was satisfied he'd taken in a sufficient amount.

Before too long, the gray tinge to his skin took on a red feverish hue, but still he did not perspire. She added more logs to the fire. Untying him, she tucked his arms to his sides and pulled a heavier blanket over him. Not knowing what else to do, she stripped her clothing and slipped under the covers beside him. Tucking the blanket around them as best she could, she added her body heat to the rest.

~*~

"Selkirk: 5 miles." Orlaith read the signpost as she rounded the last stretch of road. Her journey had taken so long. The snow bunting had left her with an idea where to go, but birds took a direct route and humans tended not to, their roads going many indirect miles between points.

Orlaith felt a growing unease. Since early morning she'd sensed a fell quality to the day. There was no other reason for it — Oonagh knew she was gone. From her vantage on this side of the hill, she could see the village ahead but the sun was setting. Leaning forward, she whispered to the horse, "Please get us there before nightfall."

The horse began to trot.

A cart man came into view on the road ahead. A shimmer of glamour enveloped her.

~*~

Jack Moody gave a short nod to the man as he passed. He looked over his shoulder at the farmer on horseback and wondered why he thought he'd seen a woman riding astride? Had the distance been so great he'd make such an error? Deciding he was indeed road weary, he gave the reins a jiggle and clucked his tongue at his donkey, "Go on Arabel, ge' us home t' our beds."

~*~

Rowan was certain his mother would know why he couldn't speak and entered the throne room, hoping to find her. Off to the side, a chair fell over with a crash. He turned and saw the Urisk with a broom. The faun stammered, "I–I am so sorry for my clumsiness, my prince." He quickly set the chair to rights and cowered.

Fearing his voice still gone, Rowan simply nodded. The faun returned to his sweeping. Rowan was drawn to the odd tilt to the creature's head. His mother had ordered the Urisk's horn broken off for some punishment or another. Until this moment, Rowan had never given her admonishments any thought at all. He'd always believed her reprimands were justified, that as mother and queen she'd know best in any situation. It felt like he was seeing the faun for the first time, and for the first time, his mother's actions struck him as cruel. Worse, he found the fear shining in the faun eyes just now disturbing. Flann feared *him*.

Rowan didn't ponder this long before his mother came in with two of her new attendants. He watched them take her orders and leave. His mother surrounded herself with vitality and dismissed or banished anyone showing age. By the look of this pair, they were barely out of their girlhood. He considered the many fae absent from court. Odd that he'd think about them now. They'd never crossed his mind before. Going to his mother, he opened his mouth to speak but not so much as a squeak came from his throat.

Her eyes narrowed and she demanded to know where he had been. Rowan shook his head. He had no words to tell her.

144

"Come with me!" she snapped. He followed her to her chambers. She opened the trunk at the foot of her bed and pulled from it a large old book with a burned back, as though it had been pulled from a fire. She quickly thumbed through the pages. Midway she stopped and read. Cupping her hands, she brought them to her mouth and spoke into them. A moment later a glowing red light formed in her palms. This she sent to him. It knocked him to his knees. "Say something, Rowan. Speak now."

He opened his mouth and once more no sound came forth.

She did her incantation again and this time he writhed on the floor in pain. She hissed, "Speak now, Rowan. Now! I demand to know if you've been with that traitorous hob!"

He mutely shook his head, putting out his hands to signal he didn't want her to do her magic again.

Ignoring him, she returned to the blackened book and reread the page. Speaking into her hands once more, she thrust the red shimmer of light at him. He rolled to and fro in agony, the red light burning under his skin. Still, he was unable to speak. Growling in rage, she stormed from the room, leaving him huddled and gasping on the floor.

Rowan crawled to the dressing table and used it to help himself off the floor. Several moments passed before he could stand, albeit unsteadily. He felt bruised and achy, as though he'd tumbled over a waterfall and been battered by rocks on the way down. Why would his mother hurt him like this? Why was she in such a rage? He caught his reflection in the mirror. His face was ashen, his lips bluish. Dragging his trembling hands over his face and through his hair, his eyes grew wide in the reflection. His hands went to investigate the rounded tops of his ears. He turned side to side, his eye on the mirror. They weren't pointed like every fae he'd ever seen in the Aos Sidhe! How in twenty-four years did this fact escape him?

Looking past his reflection, he saw the blackened book on the bed behind him and was met with an overwhelming impression that he didn't belong here.

~*~

Realizing he'd just read the same passage for the second time, Eppa sighed and closed the book. The bird had said Orlaith would arrive midday and here it was more than two hours past sunset. His unease had been growing steadier by the minute. This was compounded by the fear that she might never see her son. Lenox might not survive this night.

In his understanding, the blood poisoning of newly forged iron often killed before the sun rose on the fourth day. But rusted iron acted differently. Eppa shook his head. How either acted upon the half-blooded, he just didn't know. He went to the window and peered into the night. *Where are you, my love?*

A knock sounded upon the door. Eppa opened it to find Orlaith standing there. Without a word they fell into each other's arms. Moments passed and a kiss followed.

Billy Blin watched the reunion from the kitchen doorway. Their love light expanded until bands of shimmering rainbows danced on the edges of their blended auras. He'd always seen the love between them, though it was brighter now that they both finally admitted it was there. He wiped away his happy tears and quietly slipped out the back door to see to Orlaith's borrowed horse. Tomorrow there would be time aplenty for his own reunion with her. Tonight he'd sleep in the straw, next to a warm goat.

EIGHTEEN

The morning air had a decided winter's chill to it. Dressed in the glamour of his old crone, Billy called for the few children attending classes to take the empty seats nearest the stove. Most of the older students were away, helping with the end of the harvest.

"Pardon me, Mother Bedelia," said one of the tallest students. "Will Master Eppa be teachin' us at all today?"

Billy grinned his old woman's near-toothless grin. "Not today laddie. No, no, no, not today. Master Eppa has taken to his bed and I don't expect he'll rise until midday at least." He patted the book clutched to his drooping bosom and told them, "I'll read a chapter and then off you go. Master Eppa will see you come Monday morning bright."

~*~

Orlaith rolled into Eppa's arms. They'd been making love since daybreak, continuing their night. For the first time in decades she felt safe and happy. She yawned daintily. After hours lost in love, she was beginning to feel tired. She told him so.

"I should leave you be, but I find it impossible."

She laughed and snuggled into the crook of his arm. "Impossible?"

"Mm hmm." He kissed her temple. "Here you are here in my arms and my heart is filled with such joy, I fear I'm dreaming. I've done so before." He felt her smile against his chest.

"Then we are dreaming the same."

He confessed, "I have loved you since the day you were born, you know."

"You were but a child."

He chuckled. "It's true. As a boy, I remember confessing to Billy that I loved you. He was rocking your cradle at the time."

Her smile vanishing, she hugged him tightly and said, "I didn't know what to think. After the deaths of my parents, I saw so little of you."

"Did you know I had planned to seek your father's permission to court you?"

The smile returned. "I did not. My father loved you as a son, Eppa. He would have approved."

He nodded. "Oonagh knew I planned to ask the king. I shared my intent the night before Queen Maeve became ill. I assumed she would be happy for us. Instead she begged me to marry *her*."

"I had no idea." Orlaith's voice was flat. "But it doesn't surprise me. My sister is only happy when she causes me pain."

He kissed her lightly. "Your ancestry demands a suitor gain royal approval for marriage. After your parents were gone, I had no choice but to ask her permission. She vehemently refused and demanded I keep my distance, or you and I would both pay the price for disobedience. She informed me that if I ever allowed you to know my feelings, she'd have me put to death and you would know it was because of you."

She caressed him. "I am so very sorry." She fell silent in her thoughts, and then said, "I couldn't bear to see the changes Oonagh was making so soon after our father's passing. There was nothing I could do. She wore the crown, not I. I spent more and more time in the grove seeking peace and understanding. I met John there."

He pulled her toward him and met her eyes. Shaking his head, he told her. "For all the pain and loss and the time apart, it was meant to be that we would share our love now and not then. Neither of us shall be alone again."

"Yes." Orlaith was silent for a time. She whispered softly, "How different our lives might have been."

"You were meant to love John and I was meant to love Annabel. Their love gave us both Lenox and Janet. From the moment of her tragic birth, Janet has brought sparkling joy to my life." He rested his head against her chest and whispered his regret, "My deepest sorrow has been the loss of your child."

She gently raked her fingers through his hair. "That you found such joy brings me much happiness. As for Lenox, I know my son was raised with a true mother's love. That was his life and I loved him from afar."

He placed a kiss over her heart before meeting her eyes. He told her sincerely, "I couldn't be prouder of Lenox were he our son together." He explained what the young man had done for his daughter.

Orlaith's smile returned.

"The truth of his life will be a shock, I know. But if I know the young man as I believe I do, his heart will love you both."

"Amelia fears his reaction, not for herself, you understand. She fears he will be hurt when all he's ever known is revealed as a lie. I've no wish to cause him pain, Eppa."

He pressed a reassuring kiss to her lips. "Billy saw him placed there at Pendry, did you know that?"

She shook her head. "I did not."

"He feared the queen would harm the child so he put him with his father's family, to keep him safe, and assure he'd be raised in a way befitting the prince he is." Resting on his forearms, Eppa gently brushed her hair back. "I tell you this not to make you sad. I do so to let you see Lenox has not fully lived a lie. He has lived as his father lived. And as his mother, Amelia has loved him true. When balanced against the truth of his life, that lie is small."

"Poor Billy. For years, every time he saw me he'd burst into tears. Now I know why."

"There is more to Billy's sorrow, my love, things he could not bear to tell you while Oonagh ruled."

"Oh?"

Eppa shared everything he knew from Billy: about *The Black Opus* and the charm that drained away her parents' lives, and the fact that Billy had saved her and tried to save them, even taking from his own life's essence to prevent Oonagh from ever physically harming her again. Eppa told her how the hob had lost both ears rather than bring Lenox to the Aos Sidhe, and how Billy took from his essence again to assure Rowan would come out from under the dark enchantment. To all of this, Orlaith sobbed softly against his chest.

Eppa held her close, hoping that once her pain drained away the events they were powerless to change would stay in the past. Together, they would build a new future. He said, "You are here with us now and you're safe. But there is one more thing you should know." He proceeded to tell her about Lenox and the iron poisoning.

~*~

Rowan stared at the blackened book on the bed, where his mother had left it. She believed the book had magic that would return his voice but had walked away when the charms didn't work. After the excruciating pain she'd intentionally caused him, Rowan knew in his heart she would return to do worse. So strong was the impulse to save himself that he tucked the book under his shirt and ran to his room on shaky legs. Once she realized the book was gone, she'd be furious. He pictured the fearful faun with his remaining antler and then Billy Blin's ears came to mind. She might do anything in her rage. He must leave the Aos Sidhe.

He'd seen his mother reduce things — even horses! — to miniature versions that could be tucked into a pocket. This was another skill he didn't possess. He gathered a small pile of clothes and rolled them into a ball, then looked at the rest of his belongings, the assorted paraphernalia of a prince born of the Aos Sidhe. His life felt wrong, as if he wore the shoes of another.

~*~

Rowan ran until his side ached. He had no direction in mind, but found himself near the home of the baker, his wife Libby, and their red-haired family. Spying a shed on the edge of the field, he slipped inside, carrying the black book. The book was very old, that much he knew, that and it was precious to his mother. He paused at the thought. Calling her "mother" now felt wrong too. A mother should be warm and caring. A mother should be someone like Libby.

A shaft of sunlight came through gaps in the wall boards and there he sat. Hoping to find a cure for his voice, he opened the book and read. He wasn't prepared for the terrible things it contained. When he turned a page, he saw recognizable handwriting in the margins. Reading the queen's words withered him inside.

NINETEEN

I woke to find myself drenched in sweat and extremely sore from head to toe. Disoriented, I struggled to determine where I was. *Carterhaugh*. It was either daybreak or sunset by the dim showing at the window but I couldn't tell which. The pungent scent of rust hung heavy around me: rust over the odors of ginger and wood smoke. And underneath it all something else — something warmly scented with lavender and roses. When I realized why Janet's perfume was near, my breath caught. Her warm form was curled along the whole length of my body. Afraid to move and afraid to breathe, I lay there wrapped in cloying sheets and confusion.

The last I remembered, I'd gigged myself in the stream. Janet helped me to the bank, where I stumbled and fell. I certainly remembered the blinding pain that followed, but nothing after. Now I find us together in bed. What had occurred between then and now?

I wracked my brain for the series of events that led me here and vaguely remembered being jostled in a cart. Eppa's cart? I couldn't imagine how he found us at that secluded site, but he was there and so was Billy. *Billy*. In my haze of pain the lad was no lad at all but appeared as some creature from the pages of one of Osgood's fairy books. Why on earth would I remember the boy's appearance that way? Had I hit my head when I fell unconscious? Would that account for the odd dreams I'd had? Nightmarish dreams, in that they were inescapably filled with excruciating pain. Testing my injury, I slowly turned my ankle this way and that and was met with a hellish ache in my calf.

Janet shifted at my back and I froze. Her arm snaked around my waist and she snuggled closer. I became aware of the heat of her skin against mine. Neither of us wore clothing. Had we made love and I had no recollection of it? Again, I searched my mind. Absorbed in the wonder of how she came to be beside me, and how right it felt, I laid my arm over hers. My touch woke her. She bolted upright.

"Oh *thank* the Lord of All! The fever came."

Rising as bare as the day she was born, she lit the lamp and looked me over. Her gentle hand swept across my damp forehead. After that she wiped her hand on the blanket, so sodden was I. She asked, "How do you feel?"

I fixed my eyes upon hers, the safest place for them to settle. "Like a man trampled by a coach and four in the rain." I tried to chuckle but stopped short. My ribs ached. "I have little memory save what occurred at the stream."

Mindless of her undress, she went to the bowl and ewer and returned determined to wash the sweat from me. Between washings and wringings, she explained that I'd been very ill and she'd hoped for a fever to cure me. I'm sure she said more but the distraction she was causing to my mind muddled it all. Forcing myself not to look at her, lest I embarrass us both, I closed my eyes and tried to listen. With my one sense absent from the rest, the scent of rust grew stronger.

She stopped at my waist, covered my chest with a clean towel, and began again at my feet. I opened my eyes. Mistake it was. Good lord, was she beautiful in the lamplight. Her pale blond hair was braided, the end of it coiled upon the bed beside me. The damp curls framing her face were darker, their very ends tapered to dark gold points. The line of her body, the delicate frame, her breasts . . . Damn me, but I couldn't help my body's reaction to her. Her rainbow aura reached out and touched mine. I couldn't breathe.

I can't say how long we stayed thus, but the professionalism of her calling came to the fore. She continued on as though I wasn't standing at full staff, all the while her aura pulsed in and around me. In short order she had me trembling. Apparently this she mistook for a chill for she assured me she was almost finished and would get me under the blankets soon. It had nothing to do with being chilled and I didn't want her to stop. In fact I wanted more, much more. Upon her prompting, I rolled onto my belly and she washed my back. After, she maneuvered me this way and that and managed to get clean dry sheets beneath me.

"There," she said with a smile. Tucking a moonlit curl behind her ear, she added, "Far more comfortable than damp linens, hmm?"

I found my voice. "Quite. Thank you."

My gaze followed her to the window, where she opened the sash and poured out the basin. I rubbed my eyes. The water I saw clear in the basin when she began now appeared *orange*. I looked at the pile of linens on the floor. They too held on odd orange tint. Did the rusty stink come from some concoction she used in her treatment?

She refilled the bowl and proceeded to wash herself as though she had done so in my presence one hundred times or more. The delightfully feminine process gave me my last inch. I rolled to my belly, the action reanimating every ache in my body. Needless to say, it quickly set me to rights.

Her toilette lasted mere minutes. Now dressed for the day, she deftly unbraided her moonlight hair, brushed the cascade, and then just as deftly, braided it up again. Turning to me with a smile, she said, "Mrs. Frew has been coming each morning with tea and scones. Would you prefer something heartier? It's been four days since you last ate."

"Four days?!"

She frowned. "Your injury made you very ill."

"I can't see how my injury was so great that it can hardly be felt now." Against her caution and my own throbbing muscles, I sat up in the bed and pulled my foot across my knee to lift the bandage. Even my untrained eye could see the miracle here. The tine had gone straight through my foot, yet there was no wound on either side. For a moment, I wondered if the local gossip about her being a witch held truth. Whatever was there had been healed in a span of *four* days. I looked at her and traced the faint line above my anklebone. Prodding for answers, I said, "I'm not too simple-minded to be unable to grasp the mechanics behind my miraculous healing."

She sat beside me and refastened the bandages. She said, "I'd prefer my father speak with you. He would explain your illness and treatment better than I."

I could see emotional discomfort reflected in those violet eyes. Yes, I wanted to know how this healing transpired. Conscious of her unease, I acquiesced. Instead, I sought other answers. "I recall your father's presence at the stream. It was his cart that brought me here?"

"Yes, it was."

"Was Billy there as well?"

"Yes. Billy helped us care for you."

I didn't ask how they knew to come. Instead, I thanked her. I expected her to laugh when I lightly mentioned Billy's appearance as seen in my delirium.

Instead Janet looked uneasy.

"I thought you'd find that amusing."

She laughed, but it wasn't the genuine laughter I'd come to love.

"Something is amiss here. No, don't deny it. I see it in your eyes. Please, Janet. Share whatever it is. We are at the least friends, are we not?"

She opened her mouth to speak but I wasn't to get my answer, for Mrs. Frew knocked upon the door. The housekeeper entered with Winnet in tow, the latter laden with tea and scones.

Mrs. Frew's eyes positively sparkled when she saw me. "Oh thank heaven an' all the saints and spirits new an' auld, yer lookin' much improved yer lairdship, *much* improved! We were worrit wi' yer blood poisoning and broken bone, but we knew ye were in guid hands wi' her ladyship." She gave Janet an affectionate smile that made me smile. I could also tell the effervescent Winnet was near to bursting in her attempt to remain silent. She too was grinning from ear to ear.

I addressed the three, my eyes on my witch, "Indeed I was in good hands. My wife has restored me." I reached for Janet's hand and gave it a squeeze.

The house keeper told Winnet, "Go tell Mrs. Nevin his lairdship is

155

awake."

"Yes, ma'am." Winnet bobbed and off she ran.

To me, Mrs. Frew explained, "Mrs. Nevin has been keeping hot mutton broth on th' stove." Catching herself, she quickly added, "Oh my word. I should ha' ask if yer lairdship if ye ha' a taste for it or anything else before I sent th' girl."

I didn't favor meat broths but found no complaint in the gesture. I was decidedly weak from my mysterious ordeal. The cook's stout broth might do me good. I nodded. "Broth would be welcome, Mrs. Frew. Do thank Mrs. Nevin for her thoughtfulness. And please inform Potts I'd like a bath."

I found myself alone a short while later, when Janet left to tend Mrs. Frew's medicines. Whatever had happened during my four lost days, she wasn't forthcoming with details.

Coming in from the next room, Potts announced my bath was set. I looked at him. The man sported a black eye and swollen nose. Why on earth did my manservant appear as though he'd been brawling? I asked him.

"Er, well." He cleared his throat and tried again, "I mean to say . . . . "

"Out with it, man."

"You were in a bad way, sir. You took to fits and walloped me when her ladyship had me tie you down."

"*Tie me?* What in *blazes* happened these last four days?"

He hurried to assure me that all was fine. "I only know what I know, sir, and believe me it isn't much. Her ladyship brought you here injured. You were very ill and Lady Pendry and Mrs. Frew saw to your care. Everyone else stayed at the ready, but weren't needed. We all thought you had the lockjaw, sir, especially when the cramps set in."

Lockjaw? Was that why my muscles ached so? To my knowledge, tetanus was fatal more times than not. Before it took you it brought muscle spasms so strong, fractured bones were often the result; a horrible way to die, by all accounts.

I was about to remove my unnecessary bandaging when I caught myself. Had Potts, and lord knows how many others, seen this miraculous healing of my wound? Janet had enough suspicion cast in her direction that I wouldn't give fodder to more. I sent him on his way and examined my ankle.

The skin showed pink where the wounds had been. I knew for a fact the fork had come up through the bottom of my foot right through the top along my ankle, for I'd felt it as well as seen it with my own eyes. When I stumbled onto the bank and fell, the tine snapped off and I was met with excruciating pain the likes unknown. I also remembered that Janet stabbed there with her small knife in an attempt to dislodge the tine. My full memories ended there. The rest was naught but a jumble of recollection and delirium.

I sunk into my blissfully hot bath and closed my eyes. Met with the heavy smell of iron again, I sat up and looked at the water. Janet must have treated me with some iron-laden concoction, for my bathwater had taken on a rusty tinge.

Fragmented visions came to mind, some were truths: the gigging, the blood, the cart that brought me here. Others were bizarre figments produced by a fevered mind, such as birds flying into Janet's waiting hands. *Hands.* A strange vision of Billy materialized. I imagined his fingers draped in spider webs, fingers that clearly didn't belong to the boy I knew him to be. For an instant, I thought Billy was an old woman from my past, the same old crone who'd pulled me toward the hedge when I was a boy. My fever must have been high for *that* memory to come forward.

I flexed my foot in the water and then recalled Mrs. Frew mentioned a broken bone. Four days to heal a broken bone was unheard of. As a student of the sciences, I understood natural processes. Nothing could advance the time needed to heal such a wound, therefore something strange had occurred. The faces of the wary came to mind, those suspicious few who'd peered through their shutters when Janet and I made the rounds. Damn me if I wasn't suspicious myself. Was Janet the true witch some considered her to be? Were witches anything more than old wives' tales or fairy stories? I certainly couldn't explain my healing.

~*~

The door was still open between our rooms and there I found Janet waiting. After looking me up and down with a clinical eye, she said, "You're tired. Come back to bed."

She'd get no argument from me. The simple act of bathing had worn me out. She turned down the linens before helping me out of my robe. Some threshold had been crossed during my convalescence because here I was, standing naked before this woman, and it felt the most natural state in the world. She tucked me in and kissed me sweetly on the lips. Had I the strength to do so, I would have encouraged her to join me in finishing what began several nights past. I took her hand in mine and told her.

Those expressive violet eyes sparkled as did her rainbow aura. It reached into mine exactly as it had when she'd washed the sweat from my skin. She smoothed my brow and said, "Sleep now, dearest."

I smiled. "Dearest? Dare I hope you love me then?"

Her next kiss curled my toes. She spoke teasingly against my lips, "No."

"Little liar," I said, returning that kiss with some teasing of my own.

I went to sleep a very happy man.

~*~

Rap tap tap.

Janet's gaze shot to Lenox asleep on the bed. She hurried to the window before the bird knocked again. The crow jumped on the sill and bobbed his head up and down. Leaning close, Janet listened to the raspy chitter. She pulled back in surprise. She asked, "*When?* When did she arrive?" The bird fluffed its feathers, as if it didn't appreciate being asked to repeat the news. Sighing, Janet told him, "Tell Billy I said to give you a *whole* slice of bread upon your return. Now say their message again." The crow chittered once more. Sending the bird on his way, she closed the window behind him.

Turning, she discovered Lenox propped on one elbow with questions burning bright in his gray eyes.

"Lenox—"

"Care to explain that?"

She shook her head.

"Alright. Then explain how it is my wound is miraculously healed in a span of four days."

She bit her lip.

"No? Then come here." He patted the bed.

She sat beside him.

He said, "Do you know when it was that I first set eyes upon you?"

"In my mother's rose garden."

"No, not then." he shook his head. "I saw you at MacPhee's Peg the night I first came to Selkirk."

"Oh?"

He nodded. "The night MacPhee's son was born, I watched a goddess descend the stairs on a beam of moonlight." He took her hands in his and his rainbow-edged aura pulsed around him.

"I didn't know you were there."

"I was. I thought you the loveliest creature I'd ever set eyes upon. When I saw you again that sunlit morning in the rose garden, you completely stole my heart."

The power of his aura intensified with his confession. Janet smiled.

"I am well aware of your healing arts. I suspect your knowledge alone brought me from the brink of death. I've heard many things about your skill since my arrival. Some credit you with following the auld ways. Some say this skill of yours is uncanny. Others declare you a witch."

Her smile dimmed with the all-too-familiar accusation. There weren't many of that opinion; those who held it had highlander roots mainly. She attempted to ease her hands from his, but Lenox wouldn't let her go.

"Janet, please understand me. It matters not to me if skill or magic comes from these hands." He raised them to his lips and kissed her palms. "But my own miraculous healing has left me with questions. Do you see my need for answers?"

She nodded. He had phrased it in such a way that he hadn't actually asked it himself.

"Then please explain."

"Witches were never more than skilled healers, able to discern illness and treat it," she said, shaking her head. "The superstition surrounding these women is unfounded."

Lenox looked at her expectantly.

"I *am* a healer, Lenox, but I am not a *witch*."

Unable to tell if he was relieved, disbelieving, or disappointed, she went on, "Most people in the town prefer a physician treat their ills. Others trust the tried and true herbal medicines they were raised on. There are a few who hail from places where healers were thought to do witchcraft or magic rather than genuine treatment with herbs and roots. Rosie MacPhee's mother held that opinion of me until very recently. I simply have a deeper understanding of healing than most. I am able to determine treatment through simple observation. What seems obvious to me is often invisible to others."

Lenox nodded. "I understand. For all of my life, I have known things others do not."

Sensing an opportune moment, Janet urged him to explain.

He gave her a smile. "Animals respond to me favorably, for one. I'm also able to determine someone's health before they realize they are ill. This perceptivity lends itself to observing the health of animals and plants as well."

"Don't you find that curious, Lenox?"

"There have been times where I've wondered why I alone have these abilities."

As he did with hers, she brought his hands to her lips and kissed them. Looking up, she met his eyes. "I know what you see when you look at me, for I see the same. You see an aura, the same light of life that surrounds every living thing."

His eyes brightened. He said, "*Extraordinary.* You are the *first* person of my acquaintance who has ever mentioned this ability. I've always seen auras surrounding people, animals and plants as well. The auras of your father and Billy are unlike the rest. And when I look at you, your aura is even more profound. It's singular, *unique*. The very outer edge reminds me of a rainbow in the sky after a storm."

Choosing her words carefully, she said, "We see it this way on one another because we love. Billy calls this rainbow our *love light*. His kind sees things differently from ours."

"His *kind*?"

"Yes, his kind are different. The same as Mrs. Frew's kind is different from ours."

"I don't understand." Lenox shook his head.

Gently raking her fingers through his hair, she said, "I know you have questions, but you've only just put the worst behind you. Will you trust me a while longer? Tomorrow, *if* you're strong enough, we'll visit my father. I promise he will be able to explain so much better than I."

"And what should I do if another bird comes knocking?"

She grinned playfully. "Let him in."

TWENTY

Rowan woke with a start. It was just as well, never had his sleep been so wretched. By the pale light outside, he determined it was dawn. He looked around the dimly-lit shed and spied the blackened book filled with the truth of his life, among other things. Easing from under the horse blanket so as not to fill the small space with choking dust again, he reached for the book. He opened to the entry his mother had made in the margin. *Mother.* Rowan frowned. Queen Oonagh was not his mother, nor was he prince and heir to the Aos Sidhe. In the early morning light, he stared at the queen's own words written there.

His eyes unfocused as his thoughts tumbled. He'd had a mother once, a true mother. Oonagh had ripped him from this family and made him a changeling whose sole purpose was to die for her magic. Though he'd never knew of one personally , he knew there was a time when the fae took sickly human infants to heal and raise rather than watch them die in the elements. As far as he knew, he hadn't been sickly. Had another taken his place?

Hearing a woman's voice calling her chickens and geese, he peered through the gapped boards to see Libby casting handfuls of grain on the ground. The baker kissed her cheek and then led his horse from the paddock and rode away. Recalling the man's smile when last he saw him, Rowan felt the gap in his own front teeth with the tip of his tongue. He knew. He had Libby's red hair and the baker's smile, and every time he saw that woman, all he wanted to do was wrap his arms around her. His silent throat choked with emotion.

~*~

"WHAT do you MEAN he's NOWHERE to be found?" Oonagh shrieked into the faces of her guardsmen, "FIND HIM*! Find Rowan* or you'll wish you'd died trying!"

The guardsmen scattered.

Just that morning she'd discovered *The Black Opus* missing and Rowan along with it. It didn't take much effort to connect one to the other. Rowan had *The Black Opus* and both were nowhere to be seen. It was essential they find him. She wasn't concerned for the book, as she knew he could never destroy it, but time was running out. Samhain was not three weeks away. She had waited nearly twenty-four years for this, watching her appearance turn old and sallow. Now Rowan was gone and the other changeling was somewhere in a place called Selkirk. She had the sudden thought to make Billy Blin send out ravens to search, then remembered Billy left the Aos Sidhe weeks ago.

She walked among her flowers and noticed several fading blossoms. The silver scissors in her hand suddenly seemed too small for the task. A sparkling swirl changed them into silver shears. She counted those missing from her court as snipped and her anger grew with each.

It was an insult. *Snip*

How *dare* they? *Snip*

They *defied* me. *Snip*

I am their *queen*! *Snip*

My sister left in the night. *Snip Snip*

I'm certain that miserable hob was the reason. *Snip*

I'd wager she's with him, damn her. *Snip*

Perhaps she's with Eppa as well. *Snip Snip Snip*

Remembering Eppa's refusal of her affections all those years ago deepened her scowl. I would have made him king if not for his love of Orlaith. *Snip Snip*

Why didn't he love me? *Snip*

Her sister's perfect visage came to mind. The shearing took on a madness of its own. Furious, Oonagh growled her tirade under her breath as she hacked the healthy rose bushes down to the soil.

~*~

A young lady in waiting made her presence known. Oonagh turned from the destruction that was once her royal garden.

"P-Pardon me, your M-Majesty," the girl stammered, "C-Captain Keon of the guard asks for y-your audience."

"Send him to me."

A moment later, the man entered and bowed. He said, "Your Majesty, I regret to inform you that your son has not been found. I say with certainty: Prince Rowan is not in the Aos Sidhe or the lands above."

Drained from earlier venting her rage, Oonagh closed her eyes and took a resigned breath. *The Black Opus* was a loss but she clearly remembered the incantation she'd need to keep her beauty. The words mattered, not the book she'd read so many times. She pictured the precious charm written on the page. The words must be spoken as the throat of the sacrificed is cut and it must occur at the stroke of midnight on Samhain eve. Her changeling was gone. There was nothing else to do. She told her guardsmen, "Saddle the horses, we ride to Selkirk."

TWENTY-ONE

Twice I attempted to continue our perplexing conversation on our ride to Eppa's cottage, but both times Janet put me off with the promise that he would have answers for me. When we arrived, Eppa appeared at the door, opened his arms to his daughter, and then gave me a welcoming pat on the shoulder. "I am so glad to see you well at last, Lenox," he said. "We were all *very* worried for you."

"Thank you," I said sincerely. "I do believe I owe your daughter my life."

He beamed with a father's pride. "She is a natural healer, as was her grandmother, my mother."

Our greeting was cut short when Billy burst from the stable, beaming from ear to ear. He ran to the house with his milk pail sloshing over his clothing and shoes. I couldn't imagine what Janet meant by Billy's *kind*. The unusually bright aura aside, I saw an exuberant youth of perhaps ten years old.

When I turned back to the pair, I noticed Janet whisper at her father's ear. I imagined it must have to do with my ever increasing list of questions. This was borne out, when he said to me, "My daughter tells me you have questions."

"That I do, sir."

Janet smiled at me and I winked at her. She said to us both, "I will leave you gentlemen to your chat."

"Walk with me, son." He placed a hand on my shoulder and led me toward the gated pasture. The horses and goat made their way to us from across the paddock. Before long, the chickens followed. We stood at the rail fence facing the schoolyard. He said, "I have a few questions of my own and I beg you indulge an old man by allowing me to ask mine first."

"Of course. What do you wish to know?"

"I see your relationship with my daughter has changed."

I assured him quickly, "I love her and Janet loves me. With your blessing, sir, I would make her my wife in truth."

He turned back to the pasture. "You would understand that as her father, I would like to know more about you and your family."

I told him about the Pendry estate. He asked who I took after in looks and temperament and seemed very interested in my father and my Uncle John. I added, "As I never knew either man, I don't have a clear image to impart other than what my mother and the servants have shared through the years."

"And what of your mother?"

"I've been blessed with a devoted mother." I relayed some of her more charming idiosyncrasies.

He laughed and said, "She sounds like a remarkable woman! You are her only son?"

"Yes, though, she would have filled the house with children had she been physically able. The poor dear endured several stillbirths before I was born. I was the last, you see, born a month after my father passed. Recently widowed as she was, I can only imagine her despair had I not survived. I'm told she loved my father dearly. My mother's lady's maid once confessed they feared for her the night I was born."

"I'm sorry to hear such a gentle woman endured such loss."

I nodded. "She's a dear, if not a little over-protective. I confess I dream of Janet and me filling her arms with grandbabies one day."

I recognized joy dancing in his violet eyes and his words were sincere when he said, "That would please me as well."

I smiled inwardly at his backhanded consent to our marrying.

Patting the horse on the head, he said, "Do you ever wonder, Lenox, what fate hands us?"

I considered his words. Yes, I'd often wondered about my lot in life. My school chums seemed content enough with their allowances and their pastimes. I, on the other hand, felt out of step with the rest, as though my life were a suit coat tailored for someone else. I shared the thought with him.

He nodded. "Yes, an appropriate comparison. I don my headmaster's coat each morning, but it doesn't quite fit me either. Selkirk has been good to me, but I long to go home where I belong."

Eppa didn't say from whence he hailed and I didn't ask. Instead I watched him tear weeds from along the fence post and feed them to the horse. The goat jumped her front legs onto the rail to get some too. He continued, "I often contemplate the many paths each life crosses. It seems to me that small steps often lead to large experiences either for the good or bad."

He went on to explain how he once loved a rare and exceptional woman. He told of her tenderness and compassion, of her sweet ways and gentle spirit. They'd been dear friends as children and he loved her completely. For years he'd planned to ask her father's permission to court her when they grew old enough. On the very eve he requested an audience with her father, both of her parents suspiciously fell ill and died in a matter of days. He then told how her elder sister, as the head of the family, denied his request in no uncertain terms, and forbade him to associate with her in any way. To this he added, "The wheel of the year turned many times and all the while I loved her from afar. She eventually fell in love with another man and it was enough for me to see her happy. But the night she planned to leave with him, he was killed. She carried his child and gave birth beside his dead body."

"That's terrible."

"It was, but the worst was yet to come."

I listened as he relayed a horrific chain of events that ended with the woman's newborn infant stolen away the moment he was born. "I wasn't there to prevent either tragedy," he said. "To this day her pain remains my greatest regret."

That he loved this woman was obvious, for I felt his pain when he confessed he wasn't able to help her. Sympathizing, I laid my hand on his shoulder. An electric sensation coursed upward.

"But life continues, does it not? Had events not gone as they had, I would not have my Janet and I would not be standing here with you today."

True that. Feeling suddenly exhausted, I leaned on the gate and offered, "I am not without resources, Eppa. I would be more than happy to help her find her child. It's my understanding that London investigators are keen for such mysteries. They might learn of the child's whereabouts."

Those wise eyes brightened. He looked at me with what one could only describe as fatherly pride. He words confirmed it. "What a fine young man you are and such a generous offer. But she knows where her child has been all these years. He was raised in a safe and loving place." Eppa clapped me on the back and steered me toward the house. "I see you're fatigued. We will find answers to your questions, but let us go inside where you might rest."

~*~

Billy hurried up the stairs to Eppa's room. Seeing the door open, he entered. There he found Orlaith standing at the window. By the shimmering rainbow that surrounded her, he knew she was watching her son with Eppa. He joined her.

She turned and smiled, tears shining brightly in her gray eyes. She said, "I never expected to see him again, Billy. And there he is, so close." Her hands went the locket she wore. Opening it, she showed him the small images inside. "Amelia gave this to me, with two images of Lenox, both younger and the man he is now. I cannot believe how like his father he is."

"I thought that very thing the moment I saw him here," Bill said. "But Lenox has my darling Maeve's eyes, just as you do, my dear. I saw that too. I also see King Ruaraidh in him, especially in the way he carries himself. *And* he's as just and kind as your father ever was. Yes yes yes, he is. You'll see when you talk with him."

A tear coursed down her cheek. Billy held out his hand and a beautiful lace handkerchief appeared. Just as quickly, a chair appeared beside him and he stepped atop it, up to her height. As he'd looked after her since the day she was born, he gently dabbed away her tears.

She took his spindly-fingered hands in hers and rested her head against his. "I'll not tell him who I am."

Drawing back, Billy blinked. "Why ever not?"

"Because he has a mother's love and he loves her as such. I'll not hurt either of them with the truth."

"But dearest—"

She put up a hand to stop him from saying more, but before she could explain herself, Janet's voice came from below, "Billy?"

Worried, he said to Orlaith, "Will you not at least come meet Janet?"

She bit her lip, deciding. "Does she know I've come?"

"Yes, I sent a bird."

Orlaith looked out the window. Billy followed her gaze. Lenox and Eppa were walking toward the stable yard. Sensing she'd had time enough to evaluate whether she wanted to meet Janet, he coaxed her. "They will talk for a while. Come, dearest. I will bring Janet to you. You need not show yourself down stairs if that is your wish."

Orlaith nodded without turning away from the scene below.

A moment later Billy led Janet into the bedroom, and said, "Janet, dear, may I introduce Princess Orlaith of the Aos Sidhe."

Orlaith stepped toward Janet with both hands out in welcome. "I am so very pleased to meet you at last, Janet. *Goodness*, how like your grandmother you are! And just as lovely."

"I am so glad you're here, Princess Orlaith," Janet said, taking her hands. "I've never seen my father so happy."

Orlaith smiled. "Come, let us get acquainted while we're able."

Billy snapped his fingers and not only did a full tea service materialize in the small bedroom, but the room itself had changed into a comfortable sitting room, complete with shimmering padded chairs and footstools. Both women laughed. The hob beamed with love for the both of them.

~*~

The astute headmaster led me into his cozy home, where I took a seat by the fire and flexed my sore leg. I couldn't believe how tired I was. I was beyond tired actually, I felt oddly weak. Not seeing Janet anywhere, I assumed she was upstairs, affording us privacy.

Taking a seat across from me, Eppa said, "Shall we address those questions now?"

I began with a statement. "Your daughter is a gifted healer. I understand that much for I've personally seen the results of her care."

Eppa didn't comment. I was sure he'd have me say all before he explained anything.

Continuing, I said, "I assume you are aware of gossip surrounding your daughter." I explained the first night I saw her at MacPhee's and the comment I'd heard about her there.

Shaking his head, Eppa let out a weary sigh. "Yes, the people here do have their superstitions and more than one has directed them at my daughter for her healing skills. I find it an ignorance of the unknown."

"I am a student of botany. I understand the beneficial properties of herbs as they relate to healing. What I do not grasp, however, is how a wound pierced through the flesh, let alone a broken ankle, might heal in a span of four days. That just does not happen, sir."

"No, it doesn't." He rose from his chair and went to stand at the window. Curiously, he turned and asked, "Lenox, what do you see when you look at me?"

"I'm not sure I follow . . . . "

"I take you for a perceptive man. As such, I am interested in your every impression. What do you *see?*"

I couldn't fathom what he was getting at, but I did as he asked and looked him over with a discerning eye. The man was violet-eyed like Janet and had a slender but handsome physique. He was tall, taller than most in the lowlands. His long, straight blond hair was slightly darker than his daughter's pale locks were. He had faint silver at the temples and generally wore his hair clubbed in an old-fashioned style more suited to one hundred years ago than today. I hadn't thought much of it when I first met him, for I'd once had a French tutor who didn't give a fig for fashion and wore his hair the same. Today Eppa wore it unbound and it fell past his shoulders. I thought him perhaps forty-five years of age, though it was honestly hard to tell on his young-looking, clean-shaven face. His calm bearing was notable; one didn't often see the like of it in this world. I found it unusual. What's more, I found his aura unusual. When first we met it was bold and bright, comparable to those found in the natural world rather than those seen on the streets of Selkirk. Backlit by the sunlight streaming through the window, it pulsed with the same rainbow edge I'd seen surrounding Janet, though less bold.

He raised his blond brow.

I guessed his age. My words made him smile.

"Am I far from the mark?"

"Quite far."

When I'd made my guess, I'd factored in to that assessment what I knew of his placement here as headmaster and age of his daughter. Figuring I could only be off by a decade, I said, "Then I'd have to say you are no more than fifty-five."

"And if I were to tell you I am three times that and more, what would you say?"

I started at him. Had the man actually said he was more than one-hundred-and-fifty years old? Had he made a joke? I had the feeling he was serious. I asked him to repeat his last words which he did, adding, "My kind is blessed with long life."

My kind? Yesterday morning I'd woken to find Janet speaking with a crow. Through the course of the conversation that followed, she'd said of Billy, "His *kind* are different. The same as Mrs. Frew's *kind* is different from ours." And here her father said the nearly the same.

Eppa went to the fire to add wood. When he stooped beside me and tucked his hair behind his ear to keep it out of his way, I saw for the first time his ear had a most decided point to the tip. With a physical defect such as that it was no wonder he wore his hair long.

Billy joined us with two steaming mugs. I sniffed the contents of mine, unable to discern what the beverage was.

Eppa asked him, "What have you brought us, Billy?

"Mulled wine for the autumn chill." Grinning, he tipped his head to the mug in my hand, adding, "Yours is also a tonic meant to help you heal."

I sniffed it again. Raised on mother's blends, I easily picked out rosehips, cloves, nutmeg, and cinnamon. There were vague notes that smelled green.

Billy gave me a gamin smile and challenged me. "Oh you'll never guess! No no no, you never will."

The loveable urchin made me laugh. Picking up his gauntlet, I told them about my mother and her tea blends.

Eppa chuckled.

I took a sip. Buried in the flavor of warm mead was a subtle earthy scent. I also tasted dandelion and nettle. Another sip solidified it in my mind. I said, "Alright young man, your tonic wine consists of rosehips, nutmeg, cloves, cinnamon, dandelion, nettle, and . . . ." I sipped again. "Mushroom."

The boy's smile widened. He said, "And?"

"There's more?" Another sip found lemon balm and quite possibly alfalfa. I told him so.

Billy jumped up and down and clapped his hands.

Eppa laughed. "I think you've met your match, Billy!"

"Well done, young man." I told him, "You'll accompany Janet on her rounds before long."

The lad beamed at my compliment. I swear his ears sparkled when he said, "Drink up before it cools!"

"Billy, Lenox has questions and I am at a loss as to where to begin."

The boy looked at us from one to the other, then said, "I've always felt starting with the truth is best." A swirl of glitter formed above his head and as it fell toward the ground, the boy I knew disappeared and in his stead was an earless, thin-limbed being with long spindly fingers and a beaky nose —

the same faery tale creature from my delusion! He must have seen the shock I felt for he said, "Or is Aunt Bedelia's appearance more comfortable?"

Without warning, he became an old woman. The same old woman that tried to take me from Pendry when I was a boy!

"*What?*" I jumped to my feet.

Quick as a flash he changed back into a boy, smiling from ear to ear.

Eppa said, "Our Billy is a hob, Lenox. Though humans erroneously refer to his kind as hobgoblins, hobs are gentle folk. I find them much like Tomten."

I stared, a bit shocked. I suddenly remembered seeing Janet's ears just before I managed to gig myself in the stream. Now, I felt my own ear. I'd known this physical characteristic a lifetime. Her ears were like mine, a slightly less pointed version of her father's ears.

My head began to swim as facts tumbled forth. There was Eppa the tall, pointed-eared, ageless man who longed to go home. There was Billy the lad, who was no lad at all, but a being leapt from the pages of Osgood's fairy books. I pictured Janet bargaining with the crow at the window that morning. Janet could commune with birds. Animals were unusually drawn to me. Janet was aware of auras. So was I. My mother had no such gifts. So often I'd heard how like my father I was. I came to an unbelievable conclusion — my father had been a supernatural being. Which raised another question: What did that make me?

Weary, I sat back down and asked it.

Eppa answered. "You're exactly like my daughter — a halfling — half human and half fae."

"Is this the reason for my miraculous healing?"

"In part, yes," he said, nodding, "but Janet's skill and love for you played a role as well. You were fortunate the iron was rusted. Iron is deadly to fae and to halflings as well."

Billy nodded vehemently. "Iron kills our kind in a most horrible and painful way."

Our kind. My thoughts were everywhere at once. Trying to make sense of it all, I leaned forward and held my head. Billy rested his hand on my head and I felt an electric charge course through my body. This was soon followed by a sense of peace that descended upon me like a warm blanket.

That peace was short lived, however, as a knock sounded upon the door. A moment later, I heard my mother's voice.

TWENTY-TWO

"Lenox, darling!" Mother rushed forward and wrapped her arms around me.

And here I thought my mind a whirlwind before. Struck mute for a moment, I found my voice and made introductions.

Eppa took her hand and bowed over it. Billy did the same with a flourish. Knowing what he was now, the whole affair swam before my eyes. I shook off the dizziness.

To my mother, Eppa said, "May I offer you tea, your ladyship?"

"That would be lovely."

He patted Billy on the shoulder and said, "Come Billy, let's give Lenox and Lady Pendry some time alone, shall we?"

I watched the pair go, then said, "Mother, it's good to see you but what are you doing here?"

"I've come for your birthday, of course. The weather is fine and the countryside lovely, and I wanted to visit Carterhaugh one more time. I came here several times as a girl, you know. Imagine my surprise when the butler there said you'd come here with your wife. *Wife*, Lenox?"

Eppa brought in a tray set with tea and biscuits and informed us that he and Billy would be upstairs with Janet and to call if we needed anything. We thanked him and returned to our conversation.

"Janet is Master Eppa's daughter. She isn't yet my wife but it is my sincere hope she will accept my proposal."

She sat before the fire and removed her gloves. "I don't understand.

You've only just arrived in the lowlands."

"It's a very long and complicated story. Trust I will share it all another time. Janet is unique and every bit my match. I have no doubt you will love her as I do."

Unpredictably, Mother wanted to talk about the business particulars of Carterhaugh and the productivity of the Selkirk mill. This I found odd. Odder still, in the midst of my accounting, she suddenly blurted, "Have you made *other* new acquaintances?"

"Nearly all of Selkirk, I'd say. Why do you ask?"

She stammered, "Well . . . a friend mentioned she'd come this way and, and that she might stop at Carterhaugh and—"

Her sentence ended abruptly. My mother never was at a loss for words. What's more, she was obviously distressed and it had nothing to do with finding out I planned to marry. I then realized Eppa had given us privacy for a reason. Something needed to be said. I felt it in my gut.

Life had taken a fantastical turn in the past hour and I was desperate to understand it all. It took effort to rise from my chair, but I did. On my knees before my mother, I set her teacup aside. Her hands were cold when I took them in mine. Meeting her eyes I said, "Tell me."

"Whatever do you mean, dear?"

"The very fact you're here without Fanny tells me something is amiss. There is nothing you can't tell me. I love you without reserve."

I expected all manner of things she might tell me — your father was a fae, Lenox, or Pendry burned to the ground, Lenox — or some such thing of a magnitude that would carry her here to Scotland. I wasn't expecting tears.

"*Mother?*" Alarmed, I gathered her into my arms while she cried. "Dearest, tell me. What is the matter?"

"She's going to try to *kill* you!" she said, her voice cracking in my ear.

"What?" I drew back and searched her face for answers, "Who? *Who* will try to kill me?"

She buried her face in her hands and sobbed quietly. I took her by the shoulders, "Mother, you must explain, don't leave it at that. *What* do you mean?"

She unbuttoned her collar button and reached inside her blouse to withdraw two worn and faded letters. She gave one to me which I unfolded and read.

My Dear Lady Pendry,

I know you have been in contact with his mother. No matter. We ride on October 31st and he will ride with us.

Queen Oonagh

I read it once, and then read it again. I met her brimming eyes and she nodded wordlessly.

My earlier conversation with Eppa pushed to the front of my mind. As though my life were a deck of cards, all the suits instantly shuffled into place. I looked at my mother's face, her precious, loving, motherly, face, and I knew. I was not born to Lady Amelia Pendry. I was aware of her many miscarriages and stillbirths. The man I'd always assumed was my father died just prior to her giving birth, to *another* stillborn babe. Someone had torn me from one mother's arms and given me to another. My heart started to pound. I took the other letter from her hand and read.

Dearest Lady Pendry,

Today, at long last, my search has ended. My heart could burst with joy. We both hold dear a child, our child. His father, your husband's brother John, was murdered and the babe taken from my arms the night he was born. I know not how he came to be with you, but I am grateful, truly grateful he has his true and loving family to raise him. You are able to see him safely brought to manhood and I am not. I leave him to your tender care. Never reveal he is of both worlds — human and fae — for the truth might harm him. And you must keep this letter close always. The glamour I've laid upon it will keep you both safe.

Orlaith

I carefully refolded both letters and handed them back. Uncle John, who I resembled so strongly, was actually my father. I was a halfling, as Eppa said. But my previous epiphany was wrong. The man I long believed to be my father was not the source of that mixed blood. This I owed to Orlaith, the tragic fae who was loved by Eppa. Orlaith gave me life and gave her blessing for another to raise me. By accident or design, I was raised a true son in the house of my father. And all that aside, as far as I was concerned, *this* gentle soul before me was my mother. I told her so and she clung to me and cried out her fear that I'd reject her.

~*~

A door mouse ran along the wall and out the door. At the base of the stairs he gave a mighty jump and climbed the step. He did it again, and again. Ten steps later, he squeezed under the bedroom door.

Scooping up the mouse in his hands, Billy held him to the hole of his ear. The rodent chipped and squeaked and when he had nothing more to say, Billy set him on the floor and pulled a hard rind of cheese from his pocket. He offered it to the little fellow, saying, "Thank you, my dear. And this is for your trouble."

The mouse promptly went to work on the cheese.

Orlaith's eyes narrowed.

Grinning happily, Billy said. "Don't worry, they never saw him. He just sat under the chair and listened."

Janet said, "Is Lenox alright?"

"Oh yes yes yes, dear Janet. And so is Amelia Pendry."

Orlaith met Eppa's eyes. Asking on her behalf, Eppa said, "Does Lenox know the truth then?"

Billy nodded. "She's told him and he loves her regardless, exactly as I knew he would." Billy sat beside Orlaith on the settee and took her hand in his. With misting eyes, he told her sincerely, "You can meet your son now, my dearest. This terrible thing has come full circle at last."

She hugged him fiercely. Then they opened their arms to Janet and Eppa. The four stayed that way a while longer.

The door mouse stuffed his remaining cheese in his cheek then went back under the door to return to his home beneath the roots of the apple tree.

~*~

Though it pained us both, my mother shared what she remembered of the night I became her son. Between sniffles and hiccups, she explained she'd been widowed a month and had already lost four babies in six years; two were stillborn and two failed to thrive. I knew this story up to this point but the rest was new to me. She related that she'd heard how feeble the babe's first cry was and knew in her heart she'd lose him too. The doctor must have felt this was the case, for he insisted that she rest and the child was sent to the nursery. But she'd seen the boy, just a glimpse, enough to know he was as bald as an egg. When she woke, I was in his place — me with my shock of black hair and slightly pointed ears. She knew in her heart that her son had died. She said she had no idea how I came to be in his stead, but the moment my eyes opened and I looked at her, she knew I was hers regardless.

As she talked, I pictured the household at Pendry. Most had worked there the full length of my life and longer. Had any seen the switch and kept silent? Of course, I thought. Nothing occurred in that household without Fanny and Osgood knowing about it and both were caring and faithful to a fault. There was no possible way subterfuge of this complexity would be missed by either. Then our butler's collection of fairy books came to mind — a rather odd passion for a grown man, I'd always thought. *Had* Osgood and Fanny known but decided to shield my mother from more heartbreak with their silence? Another thought took me. It didn't matter.

I felt Janet's presence behind us and turned to my moonlit witch. Nay, I amended, no witch — a beautiful enchanted being — a halfling like myself. Never did my life make so much sense. I took Janet by the hand and introduced her.

"Mother, may I present Miss Janet Eppa Roxburgh. Janet, Lady Amelia Pendry."

Her handkerchief hastily dabbing her remaining tears, Mother stood and offered a hand.

Janet stepped forward, and taking it, said with a welcoming smile, "Lady Pendry, I am so pleased to meet you at last."

I said, "If Janet will have me, Mother, she'll soon be your daughter-in-law."

Mother laughed. After all her tears it did my heart good to hear it. She said, "Lenox darling, such a proposal!" Turning to Janet, she embraced her and said happily, "Never mind his delivery, Janet. I can see proof of his love for you sparkling in his eyes."

"I see it too, Lady Pendry," Janet replied, her words accompanied by a shimmering multicolored aura. Eyes sparkling in my direction, she nodded.

My heart near bursting with joy, I kissed her soundly then picked her up and spun her around.

The sudden urge to confess came upon me, to have all secrets banished for once and for all. I set Janet on her feet and said to my mother, "As I said, Janet is my match in every way, Mother." I repeated pointedly, "In *every* way."

Mother's eyes grew large as realization took her.

Sensing her understanding, I nodded. "We are alike, she and I."

"Amelia." I turned to the female voice behind me. A tall and slender woman of indeterminate age stood in the doorway. She was strikingly beautiful, with long auburn hair falling straight to her waist. I knew at once who she was when I saw her gray eyes, for they were mine as well. *This* was Orlaith.

With a tearful gasp my mother rushed to her open arms and both women embraced. It tore at my heart to see their bodies shudder with silent tears. Before I knew what I was doing, I stepped forward. When they parted and looked at me, I realized at once that both had feared my rejection. I took each of their hands in mine and addressed the woman who bore me, "I can only imagine the pain you experienced at your sister's hand. But that terrible past need not direct our future." I looked from one to the other. "Mother and Mother Orlaith, I would have you *both* in my life."

Wound in their motherly embrace, I only now noticed Eppa and Billy, in his true form, standing beside Janet. All three were smiling. The room was so filled with love, it were as though we stood at rainbow's end.

~*~

It was late in the night when Rowan heard the tinkle of bells. He knew that sound. Whenever the queen went riding her borrowed mount was adorned with hundreds of small silver bells. Wondering why she was riding so late at night, he rose to his knees and listened. Tinkling bells and the sound of hooves on hard ground grew louder as the riders drew closer. He peered through the shed's slatted boards as the din passed but didn't see the riders or the horses. They were invisible. He could have seen through glamour when he was enchanted, but no longer.

There was no place in this world for him now. Coming to a decision, he stuffed the black book in a sack and ran to the baker's stable to borrow his horse. He had an idea where the queen was headed.

~*~

Rowan rode hard to catch up but slowed his horse when the sound of bells grew louder. He needed to keep his distance. This wretched book would never again belong to the queen.

TWENTY-THREE

I wished I hadn't been so stubborn when Janet had suggested we take the coach that morning. I found myself deeply fatigued both physically and mentally, from rusted iron and a day of startling revelations of no little magnitude. Mother's surprise arrival had cut into Eppa's explanation of iron poisoning so I still didn't know the exact reason I felt like this. It was obvious I was still in serious state, for more than once did I sense Janet's worry directed at me. Just how dangerous was an iron infection in the blood? Knowing there were answers here about the truth of my life, I was loath to leave. Billy begged us to stay for dinner and I agreed, hoping a hearty meal might gain me a bit of strength for the ride back to Carterhaugh.

Several times over the course of the evening Billy referred to me as "the young prince." Fantastic as all of this was, I took it in stride. Truth was infinitely better than fiction. But nothing had prepared me for the scope and breadth of the truth. I was stunned to learn I was heir to an entire fae kingdom that existed not two miles from Pendry.

I was honestly surprised that my mother hung on every word said. I suspect this had more to do with wanting to protect me from my insane fae queen/aunt than anything else. I, however, saw nothing to get in a stir about. I would turn twenty-five in a matter of hours and we were nowhere near the Aos Sidhe, where mad Oonagh sat on her throne.

Coming to know Billy in dribs and drabs, I learned his relationship with Mother Orlaith and her family, *my* family, was generational. Billy Blin was hundreds of years old and devoted himself to each child born to generations of my maternal line. He never said how it all began. Perhaps one day he would share that beginning. It was heart wrenching to discover how he'd been abused at Oonagh's hand. The glittering ears I'd thought I'd seen on several occasions were, in fact, magically created prosthetics.

Knowing Mother as I did, I could tell his true form was a little off-putting to her. Though she was perfectly pleasant, her surreptitious glances his way confirmed the little hob's otherworldly appearance made her a tad nervous. His perceptivity caught on, however. Coming straight to the point, he gave her a selection of forms to choose from, modeling each. Pink cheeked, she said that it was no matter and he shouldn't go out of his way. She explained everything was all so new to her and assured him she'd become familiar in time. Billy gave her a wide, understanding smile and settled on the least intimidating figure, that of a ten-year-old boy. It was a shrewd maneuver on his part, for in minutes, I felt her relax. This skill of his, I learned, was something referred to as *glamour*.

Curious, I asked, "How exactly is glamour achieved?"

Eppa said, "All life is surrounded by a field of energy and this field is influenced by the mind. If the mind envisions, the aura takes on that form."

As a student of empirical study, I found his explanation fascinating if not a little brief. I asked Billy if his ability was limited to hobs alone.

Serving us a delicious stew of cabbage and turnips, he said, "Oh no no no, even humans once knew how to use glamour." He looked to Mother Orlaith. "Isn't that so, dearest?"

She nodded. To me, she said, "There was a time they did, long ago, before the Great War."

I asked her to clarify.

"Our people, the Tuatha Dé Danann, once lived side by side with humans. Their world was not so dissimilar to ours, for we all were children of the Goddess Danu. Together we worshipped in her sacred groves and beside her springs. When the Milesians came with their false god, the children of Danu divided. Many humans embraced the fallacy. In their disdain they sought to crush any who did not and war ensued. We left those lands and settled here. The earth magic the humans once possessed faded as new beliefs took hold of their minds."

Osgood had a book of Irish fables, and I had a vague recollection of reading in it, as a boy, about the Tuatha Dé Danann and their faery battles. I had the sudden urge to pinch myself to see if I were dreaming. This was *my* lineage — the stuff of fairytales. Instead I asked if Janet and I, being half-blooded would also have this ability.

Nodding, Eppa said, "The belief connects the mind to the energies. Belief is necessary to master the art of glamour. Any who believe can form the energy field with their mind. Glamour allows us to project what we wish humans to see of us." He tucked his hair back behind his ear, demonstrating, and suddenly the pointed tip was gone. Just as quick, it returned. He took Mother Orlaith's hand and kissed it. "Other than your royal line, Lenox, where this gift is the strongest, I've found none as adept as our Billy."

"Oh such praise!" Billy grinned.

Mother Orlaith smiled, and said, "And every bit deserving, dear friend." To me she said, "I'm sure Billy would be willing to show you how the magic is done."

The exuberant little fellow bounced in his chair. "Oh yes yes yes! Teaching the young prince our ways would be my pleasure."

Janet said, "It was Billy who taught me the language of birds."

Billy said to me, "I could teach you animal speak as well!"

Eppa laughed. "Janet has taken to it as a duckling to water. Unfortunately, I have not. I find birds to be impatient creatures."

"Practice practice, my dear." Billy jumped from his chair and cleared the table ahead of a sublime pear tart.

Mother Orlaith said she hadn't seen Billy this happy since her parents were alive. She explained that housekeeping and cooking were his way of expressing his love.

To that Eppa added, "And we'll each weigh twenty stone apiece by winter!"

Billy's delighted laughter came from the kitchen.

I looked around the table at the smiling happy faces and knew I couldn't be happier myself. I only wished I wasn't so tired. The heavy meal had only made it worse. I now felt as though I hadn't slept in days.

~*~

Rowan read the sign post. Selkirk: 5 Miles.

So that's where she was headed. He felt terrible inside. It was he who'd told the queen that her sister had traveled to Selkirk for someone named Lenox. If both Orlaith and Lenox were there, what did Oonagh want with them? A hard truth hit him. It was Samhain eve, and she didn't know where he was. She meant to sacrifice one or both of them in his stead.

It was likely the queen would kill him for interfering, but death was better than the life she'd left him with. He had nothing now; no family and no world to belong to, no reason to live. He couldn't go to Libby and tell her the fae had taken him away from her twenty-five years before. He couldn't call her "mother," as he longed to do. He didn't have a voice. Picturing his true family, he wiped a tear of frustration from his cheek, wishing his life had been what it was meant to be, wishing he could undo all the harm that evil woman had done. With a strangled cry, he spurred his horse on and followed the distant bells. There would be no sacrifice this night.

TWENTY-FOUR

Because Mother had anticipated some preternatural occurrence or another, when she arrived at Eppa's house she'd had her coachman leave her at the door and return to Carterhaugh. Now, the hour was late. As she wasn't dressed to ride, it was decided that Janet and I would return to Carterhaugh and send her coach for her in the morning. It was just as well. I'd been growing weaker by the hour. After this remarkable day, I wanted nothing more than sleep.

We said our goodnights with the promise to return the next afternoon for the birthday luncheon Billy had planned. Before my mother's return to Pendry, we'd all celebrate my turning twenty-five unopposed by a mad queen's outrageous murder plot. My sleepy mind boggled at the thought. I knew time would make sense of it all, but for now one thing was certain: the love I shared with this special woman beside me. We talked for a time and decided we'd marry some place far from here, in Gretna perhaps. The town had quite the reputation for clandestine marriages, as ours certainly would be. My words prefaced by a rather loud yawn, I mentioned to Janet how incredibly weak I was feeling.

Reining her horse alongside mine, she reached over and placed a clinical palm against my forehead. I could hear the concern in her tone when she said, "Your skin is cold again. We should have waited another day before your venturing out. Today was too much, too soon."

"I wouldn't have missed this day for the world." I took her hand and kissed it. "You'll soon put me to bed and with your tender care I'll be fine in the morning."

Janet relayed her father's opinion that it might very well take weeks before I'd be fully recovered and feeling my full strength again. She went on to explain that forged iron destroyed the structure and health of fae blood and I was saved only by the fact that I was half human and that the rust had weakened the pernicious effect of the iron that pierced me. With sudden insight, I knew it was Janet alone that brought me from the brink. I thanked her.

"What for?"

"Oh . . . for many things."

I heard the smile when she said, "Many?"

"*Innumerable* things. First, I would thank you for stealing my heart."

"I had to," she teased. "How else might I roam where I choose and pick herbs where I may?"

"Witch," I said, turning the table. "Now that I know I'm at risk each and every time I ply my steel razor to shave my whiskers, I think it most advantageous to have a skilled healer around."

Her laughter was sweet and happy. I felt her aura touch mine in the darkness and a warm, contented feeling settled in my chest. Auras entwined, our conversation tapered off to a few words here and there. I was certain her long bedside vigil had taken its toll on her as well. Before long, the hypnotic rhythm of our horses' hoof beats plied my exhaustion until I could barely sit in my saddle, let alone keep a coherent thought.

The road seemed to stretch on interminably. It was quite late when we rounded the town. All was quiet and mostly dark at this late hour. Even MacPhee's Peg was shuttered for the night with only a single gaslight burning curbside. I shifted position again. Somewhere in the back of my overtired imagination, I heard the sound of tinkling bells and hooves riding hard. An instant later the ground rose to meet me.

~*~

"Lenox!" Janet cried, as he fell to the ground. Jumping from her horse, she hurried to his side. With every ounce of strength she had, she rolled him on his back. He groaned softly. He was nearly unconscious. Patting his cheek, she tried to rouse him. "Lenox darling, come, let's get you back on your horse. We're almost home."

Janet whirled to the sound of bells and mad laughter coming from the darkness.

~*~

Her glamour fading, Oonagh pulled her horse to a halt. Voice laced with glee, she said, "Lenox? My *word*, I cannot believe my good fortune! And here I was worried we might soon be out of time. Keon, do you *know* who that is lying there?"

The captain of the queen's guard pulled his horse beside hers and followed her gaze. "I do not, my queen."

Ignoring him, she eyed the woman shielding the changeling, and said, "Step aside and you will not be harmed."

"You stay away from him!"

Had she the time, the human would pay for her insolence, but there were precious minutes left before the changeling grew too old to be of use. *The Black Opus* was very specific — Oonagh must spill his blood on an auld one's hill so the gate to hell would open. And as luck would have it, they'd just now passed such a hill. She held out her hand and a golden rope appeared. This she flung at the woman and laughed with delight as she fell to the ground, fully trussed and helpless. Oonagh couldn't imagine what was wrong with the changeling that he was so weak. He struggled to rise. She called forth another golden rope and bound him as well. To her captain and guardsman, she yelled, "Put him on the horse!"

~*~

Concealed in the bushes, Rowan overheard the exchange and watched the queen cruelly bind the pair with her magic. The guardsmen gathered Lenox's semiconscious body and laid him across the saddle of the one horse without a rider.

From the black book he knew the queen would need to find an auld one's hill for her tithe and he'd seen one not a mile back. Certain she'd go there, he grabbed the sack from the saddle and ran on foot through the trees. He *had* to get to the mound before the queen did.

~*~

Bound and helpless, Janet watched Oonagh turn her horses around and ride back the way she'd come. Janet struggled against the magic rope to no avail. Magic such as this faded in time, but she couldn't wait for that to happen on its own, Lenox was in danger. Remembering what Billy taught her, she whispered into the night for any creature to come to her aid. Her horse came to bite and tug at the magic ropes but couldn't free her. Hearing her plea, a hedgehog shuffled toward her. She told him, "Please bite through the ropes and hurry, little friend. *Please* hurry."

A barn owl called from the tree above. Janet asked him to find Lenox. The bird took off on great silent wings and returned a moment later to relay that the riders were headed to the auld one's hill. He suggested she go there directly, as a bird flies, rather than take the road. Free at last, Janet thanked them. She told her horse to bring her father and Billy then dashed off through the woods on foot.

~*~

The energy was strong here. This was where the auld ones once worshipped the Goddess, though all that remained were their standing stones. Palms down, Oonagh walked the circular mound feeling the very essence of it tingling in the tips of her fingers. She'd planned this night for so long she was giddy with anticipation. The words came easily as she drew the passage from memory and recited enchantment to call the doorway of *The Black Opus*. The outer edges of the hill began to glow with reddish light. Her hands began to take on the same eerie glow, but this magic was disturbed when the captain of the guard suddenly called out, "My queen, he's here!"

A Ban Sidhe's screech tore from her throat, "DO NOT INTERUPT ME!"

In a flash, she directed her glowing hands at her guards and knocked them to the ground. Magic fire blazed over them and they writhed in agony until they moved no more. When the human stepped into the circle, Oonagh's eyes grew wide in surprise. Too late did she realize her captain meant to tell her the changeling had come. No matter. She smiled sweetly, and said, "Rowan, dear, mother is so pleased that you've come."

His tears glistening in the light, Rowan pulled the book from the sack and clutched it to his chest.

Oonagh's eyes narrowed briefly. "You shouldn't have taken mother's book, my darling. But never mind. You are here and that is all that matters. What a wonderful night this is. When the two of you gain my wishes, I will be beautiful forever and my sister will die."

Oonagh whirled to the whinny of horses and a loud groaning thud. The human woman had come and pulled the bound changeling from his mount. There was no time for this intrusion! *The Black Opus* did not call for human blood to spill and Oonagh was loath to taint the spell with it. Overcome with rage, she flung the red magic at the pair. Instantly Lenox transformed into a snarling lion. She expected the human to scramble away in fear, but the woman clung tightly to him. Oonagh tried again. Now the changeling transformed into a huge growling bear, and still the woman held on. Again and again, from bear to boar and boar to wolf, none would frighten the human away.

Oonagh growled in frustration. Determined the human must die regardless, her palms filled with the ruby fire. Directing her malice, she was about to let it fly when a rasping voice came from behind. She spun around to find Rowan reciting from her book!

Hell fire lit her eyes. Like the half Ban Sidhe she was, she shrieked, "You fool, what are you doing?"

A burning pillar rose from the mound and split in two to make a doorway. She screamed, "Stop! STOP, I command you! NO! You will ruin everything!"

With a strangled cry, Rowan clutched the book tightly and charged at her. Grabbing her, he held her firmly against his chest, the book between them, and they tumbled through the flaming doorway as Rowan rasped his fervent wishes. An instant later all that remained was scorched earth.

Janet fell back from the wolf with a cry. The enchantment dissolved and Lenox lay panting on the ground, his clothing in tatters.

~*~

A hot blast of magical fire hit us and Janet and I were thrown into the air. I landed hard on the ground, unable to move a muscle. An instant later, Oonagh's enchantment dissolved and my body was mine at last. I heard Janet whimpering somewhere in the dark. With extreme effort, I crawled toward the sound and found her trembling in the darkness some distance away. I gathered her into my feeble embrace. "It's alright now. She's gone."

Her voice was small and her words quavered, "I was *so* afraid."

I repeated my assurance for her as well as myself. "Everything is alright now. Oonagh will never hurt any of us again."

Eppa's voice came from the dark wood. "Janet! Lenox! Where are you?"

"Lenox!" My mother's frantic voice overlaid Eppa's.

I struggled to stand. Janet jumped to her feet and called back to them, "We're here! Over here!"

The searchers came through the wood with Billy leading Mother by the hand. Sobbing uncontrollably, she ran with open arms. Nearly knocking me back to the ground, she hugged me for all she was worth.

While Janet relayed what had happened to us, Billy stood beside me, his attention elsewhere. I felt sadness emanating from him in waves. Following his gaze, I saw the bodies of the guards in the moonlight. Perhaps he knew them as they once were, before Oonagh's evil took command of them. I watch the little fellow raise his hands with a flourish in their direction. Sparkling glitter materialized and covered the bodies. To my surprise, they levitated and floated to the outer edge of the mound only to disappear under the sod.

The instant their bodies were removed, I felt a distinct change under my feet as if the ground itself could breathe free without their weight upon it. It was then I realized we stood on hallowed ground. Oonagh's dark magic did not belong here. Billy wasn't finished, however. He held out a hand and two hazelnuts glittered into being. These he poked into the soil over each grave. I don't know why, but I sensed the hazel shrubs would grow and somehow redeem the men buried beneath them.

Mother Orlaith stepped into the glowing circle of scorched earth. Palms down, she closed her eyes and called to the spirits who lingered near. At first I thought it was fireflies or swamp gasses that flashed before my eyes, but then I realized what those lights truly were. The blue mist and flashes of gold light were sprites and wisps and divas answering her summons. By god, Osgood's books had come to life, for I'd seen these beings in the illustrations. Afraid to move lest I disturb this magical sight, I watched mesmerized.

She said to them, "I call upon you to bless this place in the name of the Goddess."

The spirit energies began to circle the outer edge of light and wove between and around the standing stones. Round and round they went until shimmering blue replaced the hellish glow and the scorched earth was no longer there. They'd made this sacred hill vibrant once more.

Mother Orlaith held her hand to me and said, "Come, my dearest. Stand with me." The energetic entities rose above to let me into their swirling circle of light and I joined her there. She said, "Long ago the Goddess herself stood here. Her aura lingers still. Open your mind to it and allow your body to heal."

The entities spun around us faster and faster until everything sparkled in the moonlight, as if some unseen hand had sprinkled it all with diamond dust. The shimmer started at my feet and slowly rose up my legs. I have no clear notion how long we stayed in this magic, but I felt the shift inside me when my full vigor returned. Through that indescribable healing force, I felt one with every blade of grass, every tree and shrub, and every creature surrounding me. The woman who gave me life took my hands and added her own magnificent essence to the rest. In that instant I knew, this oneness was my legacy.

TWENTY-FIVE

Maisey Benton ran across the yard, shouting, "Papa, Papa! Jocky's come home. He's back in the paddock!"

Hearing his youngest daughter calling, Danny Benton stepped out on the doorstep. Sure enough, his wayward horse had returned. He looked the animal over with a critical eye. Several men had been talking at MacPhee's last night about their horses going missing in full tack this week. Jocky too wore saddle and blanket but looked no worse for wear.

Closing the paddock gate behind Jocky, Danny turned back to the house but stopped when he thought he heard a familiar sound at the top of the pasture. He listened. No, it was only the wind rattling the last of the autumn leaves. He turned to go but stopped mid-step when he heard the sound again. Investigating, he couldn't believe what he found at the base of the rowan tree — atop little Albert's grave — a naked infant, not hours old by the look of him. His eyes scanned the yard. Was the mother nearby? No one was there but then he really didn't expect to see anyone. In his heart he knew this was no mistake. The babe was laid here purposefully, right at this spot.

In the auld tales his gran told him, the faeries would exchange one babe for another, especially if a child was sickly. He hadn't heard of a child replaced twenty-five years later, but what did he know about the ways of faeries? His gran was a highlander and she raised him. She believed with all her soul and so did he.

Danny took off his coat and carefully swaddled the child in it. Holding him in his arms he ran a gentle finger over the soft round cheek. He was sure of it. The baby had wise blue eyes and ginger hair, like Libby and their other children. To the babe, Danny whispered, "I know you're my Albert come back to us. You're home at last, son. Shall we meet your mummy, little man?"

EPILOGUE

"Dudley, stop this instant!" Amelia scolded the portly mastiff, the dog bent on catching himself a bumblebee. Returning to the work at hand, she eyed the stack of correspondence and invitations wearily. How was it she'd been a guest at Colonel and Cornelia Parker's lovely cinnamon plantation in Ceylon these last eighteen months and *all* these people didn't know? They all knew one another for goodness sake! You'd think such gossip would fly on wings. Now obligated to write each and every one to say how sorry she was she'd missed their soirée, she shook her head in exasperation. Just two days returned and all she'd done since she walked through the door was send regrets. She set her pen down and flexed her cramped fingers again.

Thank goodness Osgood was such a capable man or heavens knew what else there might be to see to. With her away and Lenox still in Scotland, Osgood kept things running smoothly. The man was a godsend, her trusted right arm.

Sipping her latest tea blend, she took in the expansive garden. Full bloom was fast approaching. It was so good to be home for it, not that the flowers of Ceylon weren't lovely. The splendid offer made by the Colonel and Cornelia to enter the spice trade with them did tempt her, but she couldn't see herself living on a plantation half the year. She'd sorely miss her family as well as her friends. Moreover, the weather was far too hot for comfort. Still, her time in India was a grand adventure.

As she reached for her pen, she caught sight of an unusual flutter among the roses and recognized it for what it was. Turning to the lady's maid embroidering nearby, she said, "Fanny, please take Dudley inside. The bees won't leave the poor fellow alone. He's sure to get himself stung again like he did when he was a pup. His nose swelled so. Even after all that, he doesn't have the sense not to bite at them."

Fanny clapped her hands and said, "Come along, Dudley." The dog wouldn't budge. He slobbered on Fanny's sleeve when she tried to lift him to his feet. The instant she clipped on his lead, he rose to his feet. She coaxed him to follow in a sing-song voice, "That's right, who's a *clever* boy? Mrs. Comstock has a *marrow set* aside *just* for *you*."

Alone now, Amelia turned back to the rose bush. There a brilliant butterfly sparkled before turning into a note. She looked around. Satisfied no one saw, she picked it up and read the hand's glittering flourish.

My Dear Lady Amelia,

We have a most happy surprise. Do come at once. The dappled horse knows the way. Simply drop her reins.

Yours,
Billy Blin

That Billy. She set the magical letter on the table. An instant later it turned back into a butterfly and flew off. That didn't surprise her. At least Billy understood there was no hope of her ever learning to understand a word a bird said. Though she would have preferred the telegraph, after two unintelligible buntings, he sent butterfly notes instead. He really was a charming little fellow once one got past the fact he wasn't the adorable boy he appeared to be.

The first letter in her stack had been from Lenox, in answer to the telegram she'd sent from Paris two weeks ago. She picked it up and read it again,

Dearest Mother,

I've received your telegram. We're so glad you're returning home and looking forward to hearing of your adventures. We've had a few of our own. The spring festivals have ended and we're free to travel.

Your Loving Son,
Lenox

It didn't take much conjecture on her part to connect these two messages — Lenox was already in London. Believing her away, he'd gone to the fae under hill first. She couldn't *wait* to see them. In her travels she'd discovered several yards of the most luxurious purple silk for Janet. Amelia smiled, imagining how lovely it would be in contrast to the dear girl's extraordinary violet-blue eyes. And for Lenox, a mated pair of peacocks. He so loved that bird of his when he was a boy. Fanny broke her from her reverie.

"Dudley is amusing himself with a lamb shank, my lady."

Amelia tsked. "That Dudley has grown in size, while I'm not here to indulge him, sheds a culpable light on all of Pendry."

Fanny chuckled. "Dudley's a clever spoiled pup, is what he is. Mrs. Comstock said he was underfoot the entire time we were gone. But she doesn't mind him. She's very fond of the dog. Mr. Osgood caught her making buttered toast for him."

"And Lenox blames *me*." Amelia laughed. Returning to the house, they met the butler in the hall. Amelia told him, "Osgood, please inform Hodges I'd like the gray saddled."

Osgood tipped his head. "Yes, ma'am." His eyes followed her up the stairs. After dispatching a nearby footman to the stables, he turned to Fanny with brows raised.

She shook her head. "I can't imagine why she'd take that horse, madam prefers the smaller bay mare."

He shrugged. "Perhaps she just misses her son. The gray gelding belongs to him."

Fanny broke into a smile, and said, "I saw the letter from Master Lenox. It doesn't say when he'll be home, but he *is* coming."

"That's very good news." The butler smiled. They all missed the young sir.

~*~

Giving the horse free rein made her uneasy, nonetheless Amelia dropped them, as Billy had instructed. In that instant, the horse stepped off the road and trotted across the open field. As he set off with purpose, she trusted the animal would know the way, for she'd only been to the fae world once — for Orlaith's coronation — and she had no idea how to retrace her steps. A short while later the horse brought her to a large grass-covered mound.

From the outside, the Aos Sidhe appeared a grassy knoll ringed by enormous trees. But in reality the mound was a clear crystal dome covering a rather large underground city where, she was told, the entire fae population east of London dwelled. It was hard to believe such a place existed at all, let alone so close to Pendry. Unusual creatures lived there, beings Amelia once regarded as characters in fairytales. Not fully understanding the mechanism involved in the domed ceiling, her concern that the horse might fall through had her dismount. She cautiously walked to the mound, her eyes searching for the sparkling doorway concealed by magic. The very air tingled here.

"Amelia, it's so *good* of you to come!"

She turned to a familiar voice and found Billy, in boy form, looking every bit the scamp. Amelia watched the fascinating exchange when Billy took the horse by the reins and said softly to it, "Thank you for bringing your mistress." He pulled an apple from his pocket and handed it to the gray, adding, "This is for you, my dear."

The horse munched loudly.

Billy patted him, and said, "We wouldn't want all of Pendry to worry their lady lost her mount and needs assistance, so be sure you don't stray back to your stable. Stay in the meadow."

The horse stomped its foot and blew loudly.

"No, you mustn't enter the oat field."

The horse's long tail came around to swat the hob.

Billy clucked his tongue at it and chided gently, "None of that, now. You know as well as I the oats are worth the wait, my dear. I have it on good authority the hay in the meadow is very sweet this year. Besides, I'm certain Lenox will come out to see you there."

The horse nodded and walked away.

Turning back to Amelia, Billy shrugged and said, "The young prince's horse has always had a mind of his own."

Amelia returned the smile. "So Lenox *is* here."

"Oh yes yes yes, and he's not alone." He held his arm for her and said, "Shall we go inside?"

No sooner had Billy said the words when a sparkling doorway appeared. He led her through it and after walked her through several beautiful rooms and gardens. "As you can see, we've undone much of the damage wrought by Oonagh. The Aos Sidhe is as it should be."

Amelia took it all in. When last she was here, the place looked bare and tired by comparison. As happy a day as Orlaith's coronation was, the visual traces of the last queen's madness colored the fae city. It was completely changed now, everything around her pulsing with a happy vibrancy. Even Flan, the unusual goat-man she'd met here the last time, was cheerful and sporting new horns. She mentioned this difference to Billy.

He fingered his own non-sparkling ears in illustration and explained how the magic of *The Black Opus* was completely undone, adding, "One can do much when love is involved. Love is the true magic of the world, both yours and mine, my dear." Both turned as a familiar voice came from behind them.

"Mother, there you are!"

Amelia spun around. Smiling from ear to ear, Billy opened the door to the queen's chambers and slipped inside.

Lenox opened his arms to his mother and she rushed forward to embrace him. Leaning back, he swept her a glance from head to toe. "You look no worse for all your jungle gallivanting."

She laughed and said, "There will be time enough to tell you my adventures, for now how are *you*, my darling?" She looked over his shoulder, "Janet is with you, surely?"

"She is. We'll see her shortly. I have sad news I wanted to share before we see the others."

"Oh?"

He nodded, "Our Mrs. Frew passed away in her sleep this past March. The old dear had a long-standing heart condition."

"I am sorry to hear that. Glynnis Frew was there at Carterhaugh from the time I was a girl on holiday in the lowlands. Such a competent woman, she will be missed."

"Indeed on both counts. Mrs. Frew was near a mother to Janet and her failing health was our main reason for staying at Carterhaugh this long. I want you to know I plan to keep Carterhaugh and, to that end, I've hired the brothers MacPhee. Malcolm is now the estate manager and his brother Colum manages the tweed mill in Galashiels. The brothers both have fine heads for business and Malcolm knows the tenants well."

Amelia brightened. "I trust you know what's what, dear. Oh do tell me the hiring of these men means you're returning to Pendry."

Lenox smiled. "We are. Now that I've brought you up to date, there are some people I'd like for you to meet." He opened the door and led her inside.

There Amelia found Queen Orlaith and Eppa her consort standing with Janet. Orlaith came forward with open arms, and said, "Amelia! I am so happy you've come."

"As am I!" Eppa greeted her with a hug of his own.

Janet embraced her warmly as well, and said with a smile, "Mother

Amelia, it's so good to see you! Lenox and I can't wait to hear of your adventures in Ceylon." Affectionate greetings were exchanged all around.

Lenox called to Billy in the adjoining room, "Billy, would you join us please?"

Billy entered the room, cradling two swaddled infants in his arms.

Amelia looked from Billy to Lenox and Janet. "What's this?" She felt for the chair behind her, her legs feeling suddenly weak.

Lenox smiled. "Mother, I'd like to introduce you to your grandchildren." He took the babies one at a time and set them in her waiting arms. "This beautiful little girl is our daughter Annabel. And *this* handsome little fellow is John Evan, the 11th Earl of Pendry."

Amelia looked down at the precious bundles in her arms. The twins were black-haired like their father but both had their mother's extraordinary violet eyes and the slightest of points at the tips of their ears. Such beauty she never beheld. Her eyes filled with tears of joy.

~*~

I watched the new grandparents coddle the babies. Three happier people did not exist, except, perhaps, for myself. As we'd arranged for such, Mother went on a tour of the Aos Sidhe gardens with the promise of blooms the like the world above had never seen.

After the babies' feeding, Billy put my son and daughter in the same nursery bed he'd fashioned for Mother Orlaith all those years ago. It was an extraordinary piece that looked as though he'd simply asked the tree to form into a cradle and it had. I watched him rock the cradle slowly and within seconds Annabel and little John fell fast asleep.

With my mother obviously softened to his true appearance, Billy returned to his natural form. That he still considered her sensibilities touched me. What a kind and gentle soul this little fellow was. Through Janet and her father, I'd learned the terrible part Billy played in the tragedy surrounding my birth. It was his bravery and cleverness alone that kept me safe — out of

Oonagh's hands — and allowed me to be raised in my father's home. He'd watched over Mother Orlaith and my grandmother Maeve, and I learned from Eppa the depth of sorrow he'd felt that he could only watch over me from afar. I'd grown very fond of him.

I met Janet's eye and she nodded. I said, "Billy, Janet and I would ask you an important question."

He looked up at us, curiosity bright in his large brown eyes.

Janet said, "Yes Billy. We ask that you watch over our Annabel and John always, just as you watched over Orlaith and Maeve."

He gazed lovingly at our children and his aura beamed rainbows of the love he felt. Those long spindly fingers gently smoothed the midnight silk on their sleepy little heads, and he whispered, "I shall."

THE END

About the Author

Known for crafting characters that stay with you long after the last page has turned, Rose Anderson is a multi-published award-winning author and dilettante who loves great conversation and delights in interesting things to weave into stories. Rose also writes across genres under the pen name Madeline Archer. She lives with her family and small menagerie amid oak groves and prairie in the rolling glacial hills of the upper Midwest.

Website **http://calliopeswritingtablet.com/**

Find more great titles at:

www.indieartistpress.com

We hope you enjoyed the debut title of Madeline Archer.
If you enjoyed The Changeling, please consider leaving a review at
your favorite online venue.

You can find more books from Madeline Archer writing as
Rose Anderson below:

Hermes Online
Dreamscape
Loving Leonardo
Loving Leonardo-The Quest
The Leonardo Chronicles
The Witchy Wolf and the Wendigo
(Ashkewheteasu Book 1)
The Witchy Wolf and the Wendigo
(Eluwilussit Book 2)
Enchanted Sky

www.ingramcontent.com/pod-product-compliance
Lightning Source LLC
Chambersburg PA
CBHW072056170626
46813CB00004B/1375